# DEVIL'S SANCTUM

## T.A. Berkeley

# PRAISE FOR *VIRAL* FROM READERS

"Swift and captivating, T.A. Berkeley's debut novel grabs you from the beginning and doesn't let go as it pulls you along for an eerie and exciting ride!"

"Delicious horror-mystery with plenty of paranoia and psychological mayhem to breeze right through without putting it down."

"Such a fun summer read! … The writing is lean and moves quickly."

"A great, fun thriller (with some saucy bits in there too) that kept me guessing to the end!"

For B.A. and T.N., always and forever

# CHAPTER ONE

The swelling chorus of a seventies soul song followed them off the dance floor and through the bar, out into the clear Seattle summer night.

Pleasantly buzzed, Brandon held Nasreen's hand as she led him down the street past bars and restaurants festooned with neon signs. Sometimes if he squinted, the lights made a temporary halo around her shiny, perfect bobbed hair.

The music from each club ebbed and flowed as they passed; occasionally a street musician's drum or guitar took over. Their progress was slowed by groups of roving partiers. Nasreen saw a quiet spot under the awning of a closed establishment and pulled him over to it.

"You were kind of feeling it tonight, huh?" she said, half joking and half admiring. "Where'd you find those moves anyway?"

Brandon looked serious. "I've been meaning to tell you something." He pressed his lips together. "I went to the doctor and, well, I finally did it. I got that second left foot surgically removed."

Nasreen's face had actually started to look concerned for a second. Now she groaned and rolled her eyes, but laughter bubbled up. She slapped his chest. "Brandon! Ugh."

Pleased with the effect of his lame joke, he looped his arms around her, feeling the contours of her waist through her thin clinging dress and light cardigan. His hands trailed down to rest where her hips swelled out from there. She relented and slid her arms around his neck, stroking the short, nearly shaved hair at the nape of his neck—a gesture that had come to feel familiar in the two months they'd been dating. He *had* gotten more comfortable dancing in that time, he reflected. It helped that she never made fun of his awkwardness. He'd felt horribly self-conscious at first, but she loved to dance so he kept at it, and tonight he'd actually found himself enjoying it.

He leaned toward her, resisting the urge to kiss her on the mouth just yet, reluctant to interfere with the perfection of her glossy wine-red lipstick. Instead he trailed his lips lightly down her cheek and jawbone and lingered on her neck, which she offered up to him by flinging back her head. She was nicely tipsy, too. It was to be the best night he had for a long time after, and it was going to end much sooner than he realized.

"Where to now?" Nasreen murmured, as he stopped kissing her and pulled back to gaze into her face.

"My place?" he said hopefully, and she laughed, the silky welcoming laugh that meant she was in the mood too. But she shook her head, still smiling.

"One more drink somewhere. Then we can go."

They stepped back onto the sidewalk and straight into a group of revelers. One man, who had been walking backward for a few paces so he could shout-talk to his friends behind him, stumbled heavily into Brandon, and both of them fell to the pavement. Brandon largely cushioned the other man's fall and got the wind knocked out of him as a reward.

The inebriated man, who looked about ten years older than Brandon, leapt up quickly but clumsily. "What the fuck, asshole?" he demanded, leaning toward Brandon, who was brushing himself off and getting his bearings. As he straightened, the older man flinched back a little, seeming to realize Brandon had about four inches of height on him and lean but ample muscles to boot. Then, with a certain look of pained inevitability, the man regained his combative posture, thrusting out his chest and jaw.

"Wow," said Brandon. "You all right?" He laughed and rubbed his elbow ruefully.

"Karma got *me* right in my funny bone." He held his hand out. "Sorry, man."

The man's eyes darted side to side, and relief dawned as he took the out. "Hey, no problem, just be more careful, all right?" He gripped Brandon's hand then rejoined his companions, his boastful tones ringing out clearly even if his words were lost in the crowd.

"Are *you* all right?" Nasreen asked. Brandon shrugged, eager to forget the incident and recapture the mood. His elbow and dignity quickly recovered as she ran her hands lightly over him in a concerned way that made his heart beat faster.

They wandered farther, fingers laced together, until they reached a bar with a patio overlooking Elliott Bay. They took their drinks to the edge.

"You could've had some excitement back there," Nasreen said, resting her elbows on the low stone wall and gazing out at the water. "You really cut that asshole some slack."

"I guess," Brandon said. "To be honest, I'm not even sure I remember how to throw a punch. I haven't been in a fight since like sixth grade. Even then, the whole time, I kept wondering how the hell I got into it, and promising myself it was the last."

"Really?" she said. "See, and I thought gym teachers were screened for macho-ness before they got the job."

Brandon laughed. "Well, you know how some people can beat a lie detector? I somehow pass as someone people don't want to fuck with, even though I'm eminently fuckwithable." He shrugged. "It's a gift."

Her peal of laughter was carried on a sudden gust of wind. Brandon's short blond hair ruffled only slightly, but Nasreen's shiny black chin-length hair was becoming tousled. She tossed it out of her face and sipped her cocktail.

"I guess—I mean, maybe it's a little disappointing, you know, that I'm not a fearless protector, huh?"

"Not to me," she said, and her eyes when she looked back at him were tender. "Don't ever change, cutie."

She shivered minutely as the breeze kicked up again, and Brandon stepped behind her, wrapping his arms around her and pulling her against his warm chest. "Did you win?" she asked.

"Huh?" The feel of her against him, hips moving slightly and invitingly, sent tingles through his body.

"Your last fight. Did you win it?"

He pressed his lips to her hair as he thought back. "I guess. He ran away with a bloody nose, I got suspended. Is that winning? To me, fighting always felt like I'd already lost. I always wondered why being into sports meant being expected to get into pissing matches over nothing, you know? I guess that's why I like teaching little kids."

"Fewer pissing matches?" she said.

"Or at least easier to break up with jokes or shiny objects," he replied, and she laughed again.

Something made him hold her even tighter, a satisfied sound escaping his lips. "Nasreen," he whispered.

"What?" she responded.

"Nothing," he said. "I just like saying your name."

She turned to face him, her dark eyes shining. He drank in her features, her smooth skin, and now he gave in to temptation, claiming her lips in a lingering kiss.

"You're so sweet," she said when their lips had separated again. She traced the outline of his face from his forehead along his hairline and the contours of his jaw down to his chin, at which point he impulsively ducked and kissed her fingertips. She sighed, mostly happily but with something else underneath.

Brandon reached for his drink, which he'd absentmindedly placed on a high table beside them, and drained the rest of it. He felt a moment might have been lost, but he pressed on with something that had been on the tip of his tongue all night. "Would it … be too soon to say this?"

She watched his face uncomprehendingly. "Say what?"

He hesitated just long enough that the possibility began to dawn on her as he said it, a bit haltingly. "I … love you?"

Her breath caught in a light gasp, she turned away from him again, and he felt a sinking sensation. He found himself babbling. "It hasn't been long enough, I guess, but I've never, I feel so comfortable and … excited at the same time. I know I should … have … not said that."

She turned back around, and her eyes were still warm. She took his hands in hers. "Cutie," she said tenderly. "I didn't say that. I don't think it's too soon to be feeling that. I just …" she trailed off, lost in thought. "People mean different things when they say it, you know?"

Brandon considered that for a moment, nodding dubiously. "I guess so." But his eyes searched her face questioningly.

She looked away, then nodded and took a deep breath as if she'd weighed a choice and come to a decision. "OK. OK. Yes. Brandon,

there are a few things we should talk about."
She caught his expression and smiled. "Don't
look so worried! It's just—you deserve to know
me better if you're feeling this way. And if you
still do, after we talk, we'll figure out what you
mean when you say it, and what I mean when I
say it." She ran her hand longingly down his
chest, over his flat belly, and hooked her
fingers in his belt loop, tugging him slightly
closer to her.

"Wait," he said, hesitantly, "does that mean
you're saying it too?"

Nasreen laughed, and he melted inside. She
downed the rest of her drink and set the empty
glass down next to his. "Let's go now, OK?
Your place," she added with eyes sparkling.

He followed her partway, then remembered
he'd opened a tab at the bar. "I'll meet you
outside," he called after her, and she waved
acknowledgment without looking back.

He nudged through the people lining the
bar and nodded to the bartender. Less than five
minutes later, he was pocketing his card and

receipt and winding back through the crowded room toward the street.

He expected her to be right outside the door, but she wasn't. He scanned nearby faces and then turned his gaze farther out.

There she was, across the street, standing next to a car—a black SUV. Her little dress with glints of silver against the black, her high-heel sandals, her silver clutch in one hand all caught his eye. A man stood with her by the open back door; another sat in the driver's seat looking straight ahead. Brandon didn't recognize either of them. Nasreen's back was to Brandon, so he couldn't see her expression. But the set of her shoulders was markedly different from her posture of a moment ago. Her head was held stiffly, alert, still.

Brandon started across the street toward her, slowly, hesitant. Something about the way she was standing seemed to warn him away. He told himself that was ridiculous and kept approaching, fixing his face into what he hoped was a friendly, open expression in anticipation of being introduced to the men.

Without warning, Nasreen ducked and got into the back seat of the car, and the man got in after her. Brandon froze in surprise, then called her name. Heads turned toward him in the crowd but he didn't care. The door shut and the SUV peeled away. As it did, the man in the back seat looked out with a pale, set face, and his eyes locked with Brandon's for a brief moment that seemed to last forever. Then the car was gone, carrying Nasreen away.

# CHAPTER TWO

Brandon was rooted to the spot for a few more moments, and by the time he started loping clumsily in the direction the car had gone, it was too late. The night had swallowed it.

He ran a while longer, not knowing what else to do. His stomach felt like lead, his feet heavy and uncooperative. After a few blocks he stopped and replayed what he'd seen. Although she'd gotten in seemingly willingly, the stance of the man who held the door had felt threatening. Her sudden stillness as she stood, so different to how she normally was—how she'd been all night until then—had unnerved him. The cold, serious men, the way the back seat passenger's eyes had bored into him—it was all wrong.

He made a sudden decision and ran back the way he came, to about where the car had sat idling. He started asking people nearby, shyly at first, then more urgently, if they'd heard or seen anything unusual. Most of them probably hadn't even been there—how many minutes had he stood frozen; how long had it taken him to stumble the few blocks away and back again?—but whether or not they had been, everyone either shook their heads, demurring quietly, or avoided his gaze and walked past him without answering.

He pulled his phone out and called Nasreen but, as the ringing cut off almost immediately, leaving him listening to her voicemail message, he remembered she'd checked it earlier and remarked that it was about to go dead. He mumbled a message nonetheless, wondering where she'd gone and asking her to call him.

He wandered the area aimlessly but urgently. He searched faces and cars. His mood veered from uneasiness to outright panic as he relived the moment again and again. He wheeled around on a corner, his eyes moving frantically in all directions. He recalled the warm anticipation he'd been basking in as he left the bar, and it felt foreign and faraway.

The fog of his buzz was clearing rapidly, and the streets of Seattle looked cold and menacing around him, the people who had been his partners in revelry a monolithic mass separate from him, indifferent to his plight.

* * *

The Devil was in a mood, and everyone who couldn't leave his immediate vicinity tiptoed around him with hushed dread. The man required to stay closest to him clutched his phone and tried not to check it every thirty seconds. Each time he did, the Devil was reminded of time passing, and his glare intensified.

The Devil had never felt seriously threatened before, and now that he did, he blamed everyone but himself. The man wasn't so sure the Devil didn't deserve a share of it, but there was nothing to be gained from airing that particular point of view. Nor was there any hope of defusing his anger with the usual tools—flattery, an ice cold vodka, a pretty boy. Nothing could distract him from the object of his vengeful fury.

The phone vibrated at last and the man jumped imperceptibly before bringing it to his ear. He felt the Devil's eyes bore into him but avoided returning his gaze. "Yeah?"

"It's done. We got her."

The man's eyes flared with hope and the Devil sat bolt upright when he saw his expression.

"You did? No trouble?"

"No trouble."

He was practically trembling with relief. "No one saw you take her?"

The phone was silent except the faint sound of the car engine in the background.

"Hello?"

"No, we got away clean," the voice on the other end finally said. "It's over."

The man exhaled and put the phone down. An incredulous grin stretched his face as he looked over at the Devil. All was about to be right again in his universe.

## CHAPTER THREE

Brandon stood by the counter for what felt like hours under sickly fluorescent lights, trying to catch the eye of the humorless woman behind the desk, but in between fielding phone calls she busied herself with her computer and ignored him.

At last a uniformed policeman emerged from a door in the back of the lobby and strode up to Brandon, prominent belly leading the way. He put his hand on his belt, breathing heavily, tapping his gun with his fingers. "So you're the one that wants to report someone missing?" he said. Brandon already felt dismissed by the man's tone of voice, but collected himself.

"Yes, well, I think it was a—I think she may have been—kidnapped," he said. The incident flashed before him again and he almost groaned. "See, I was in the bar and she left right before me—"

The officer exhaled sharply. "In a bar? I'll say." He shook his head and stepped back. "You smell like a brewery!" He moved in again, seeming to tower over Brandon though they were roughly the same height. "You drive here?" he said menacingly.

"Uh," Brandon said, "No? I mean yes." He'd eventually gotten a cab and taken it to his home but, after a few minutes of pacing and panicking, had soon come back out to the police station in his car. "But it's been a while since I drank—I'm totally sober." He tried to regain control of the conversation. "Listen, I'm really worried about my—the girl I'm dating. She didn't look right. I don't think she knew those guys."

"That so?" the cop said, a sneering undertone in his voice. He shifted his weight. Tap, tap, tap went his finger on his gun again. "You say she left the bar first and you went after her, is that correct?"

"Well, yes, but only because I had to pay," Brandon faltered.

"Why didn't she stay with you then? Sounds to me like she may have wanted to get away from you. You two have a fight or something?"

"No!" Brandon said, and the sharpness in his tone seemed to make the officer bristle. He tried to walk it back. "I told her to go ahead; it was just going to take me a second and it was crowded in there. We were having a good time. A really great time." He heard his voice start to take on a quaver and paused to try and get it under control.

"OK, so you thought you were having a good time," the officer said. "And then this lady that likes you so much, having such a good time with you, she heads out and gets in a car with a couple of guys you don't know. That right, sir?"

"Well …" Brandon hesitated.

"'Cause I just want to make sure I'm getting your statement accurate, sir," the officer said.

Brandon felt like he was getting drunk again. His head spun and his ears were ringing. "The guys in the car," he started again, stumbling over his words. "The way the one looked at me, I just got the feeling they were bad news."

"So the guy your lady ran off with was giving you a look," the officer said. "Gee, do you think she maybe told him you were a creep and she wanted to get away? You think he was her friend and not too happy with you right about then?"

"No, that's not how it was at all!" Brandon burst out. He took a quick steadying breath. "Please, I need your help. Can I just give you her name and description so you guys can keep an eye out for her?"

The policeman was shaking his head even before Brandon was finished speaking. "I'm sorry sir, but we don't start investigating disappearances of adults until they've been confirmed missing for twenty-four hours at least." His voice became marginally less threatening, taking on a patronizing tone. "Look kid, I don't think you're a bad guy. I believe that you think something went down tonight, but looking at it as an outside, *objective* observer, I can tell you that it just sounds like the lady had enough of you for now, and called her friends on the way out of the bar. Now if she was abducted, you think she'd have screamed, or put up a struggle, or at least tried to look for you before she got in the car. Right?"

As the officer spoke, he was ushering Brandon toward the door. "And I'm not saying she's gonna be sick of you forever, friend. OK? Maybe you had a little argument, maybe you didn't. Maybe the lady was mad at you and you didn't even realize. You know how often that's happened to me? Hell, to every guy that's ever lived, right? Who knows what they're thinking half the time? But then a lot of times they forgive you for whatever it was, just like that. She might come around."

They'd reached the door of the station and the policeman held it open. Brandon hesitated, but he didn't see any chance of being taken seriously. He also felt a rising urge to punch the cop, or shake him, and he didn't think that would go well.

The officer made a show of sympathy, his tone artificially pleasant. "Look, she doesn't show up in a couple days, ask around with her friends. If anyone else is worried about her, give me a call." He pulled a card out of his chest pocket and handed it to Brandon, who took it with numb fingers and looked down at it with unseeing eyes. The man's belly seemed to block his re-entry into the station anyway, so he backed slowly away and headed to his car.

On the way home, he gripped his steering wheel until his hands ached and tried to replay the scene without focusing on his panic at the time. *Objective observer*, he thought.

The car—what kind had it been? He remembered black, not a make or model. A four-door, an SUV, that's all he was sure of. Had he glimpsed the license plate as it pulled away? He tried to retrieve it from his memory, but knew he'd spent those last split seconds that the car was in view trying to glimpse Nasreen through the back window.

What about the men? He could only remember their pallid complexions. He thought harder and conjured up a thin mouth set in a grim line, small deep-set eyes that glinted under frowning eyebrows. That was the man who had ushered Nasreen into the vehicle. As for the man driving, a receding hairline was all that stood out. Brandon slammed his hand on the steering wheel. With no one around, he no longer tried to suppress a groan of despair.

If the policeman's theory was true, it would be a relief compared to his dire interpretation of the event. But if it were, it would call into question everything he felt about Nasreen. She was so frank, so direct; with her, there had never been any playing games or hiding what she thought or felt. In fact, hadn't she been preparing to open up to him even more when they got home?

Of course, he hadn't known her very long. But so far, he'd never sensed any tension or discord between them. She'd given no sign of being annoyed with him tonight either. He remembered her subtle gyration as he pulled her back against him, minutes before she left the bar, and his gut lurched painfully.

He pulled up in front of his small rented house, turned off the ignition, and leaned his head on the steering wheel for a second. He dragged himself out of the car; his adrenaline was still pumping but his nerves felt strung-out from it and exhaustion was setting in. He'd tried her number over a dozen times that night, getting her voicemail every time. He always hung up quickly. Part of him wanted to hear her voice, but listening to the same message over and over just made her feel farther and farther out of reach. He couldn't help but wonder if it was the last he'd ever hear of her voice, and that thought made it unbearable to listen to it.

As he got to his door, he noticed the night sky was a slightly lighter gray. He hadn't seen the beginnings of daybreak since grad school, at least five years ago.

He pulled his keys from his pocket and unlocked the front door. He couldn't help remembering so many late nights this summer fumbling distractedly with the door as Nasreen stood close to him, nibbling and whispering into his ear, pulling at his shirt if it was tucked in, working the buttons open if it had any. She made him feel so much more attractive than he'd ever imagined he was to women. Past girlfriends had been harder to read, often leaving him wondering if he was doing the right thing or if they were really that attracted to him. Nasreen had blown up all his assumptions about women, and about himself. With her, once he got over his initial anxiety, he felt confident, adventurous, wanted. She intoxicated him. Every night they'd spent together had deepened their hunger for each other.

Or had it? Chemistry was mutual, but he suddenly felt unsure it had been there on her end. Could he have been wrong—his biggest misunderstanding of a woman yet in a lifetime of not-quite-right relationships? He never would've thought so before, not for a second, but now, when the alternative theory was so terrifying, he almost wanted to believe it, painful as it would be. He'd rather have her safe and not in love with him than be the woman he thought she was—the woman of his dreams—and be in peril.

# CHAPTER FOUR

He woke with a start to sun streaming in through the blinds of his bedroom window. He'd remained exhausted but sleepless as the sky slowly lightened outside, his body tense, his arms crossed over his stomach as he lay across his bed, fully clothed, in a semi-fetal position.

He didn't remember exactly when he'd finally fallen asleep, but a glance at the watch he was still wearing told him it had probably only been about two hours ago. Nonetheless, he had the nasty feeling of having overslept on a school day. It was seven-thirty, which would've been cutting it close for getting ready to teach, but he didn't usually feel like this during the summer months. His inner clock adjusted quickly and he enjoyed an extra hour of sleep most days. With Nasreen in his life this summer, sometimes it was more like two or three extra hours. Sometimes she'd have already crept out by the time he woke up; despite his pleas that she wake him up to say goodbye on mornings she needed to leave before he was awake, she continued the practice, telling him he looked far too angelic to disturb when he was sleeping.

But today he was all off. Every nerve ending seemed to ache from the constant stress of the night before. He fished his phone out of his pocket and called her again. Straight to voicemail. "Hi, you've reached—" He hung up, breathing heavily.

He rummaged through his kitchen cupboards—he had no desire to eat, but his stomach felt like it was grinding against itself, it was so painfully empty—and found a granola bar. He longed for coffee but couldn't imagine making it, so he found a Coke in the fridge. He carried them out to his car.

Munching glumly on the bar without tasting it, he drove to Nasreen's apartment building, an older brick structure about three miles away from his house. He hadn't been inside very often but had picked her up enough times that he didn't have to think about how to get there.

He found a spot to park across the street, then went up to the door. He pressed the code to call her apartment, imagining for a moment that he'd hear her satiny voice, ever so slightly distorted by the poor-quality speaker, telling him to come on up. But instead the buzzing ring trilled four or five times before shutting off. He frowned, stepped back, and squinted up at the window he thought was hers—he'd never really paid attention before. Then he moved in again, pressed the code again, waited, got the same results.

"Hey, man," someone said behind him, and he turned. It was one of Nasreen's neighbors, a shaggy hipster kid he knew only as Buddy and had only ever paid attention to because he could see the way he looked at Nasreen when he thought neither she nor Brandon was looking. The young man's eyes seemed to change a little as he saw Brandon's face. "You OK, dude?"

"Yeah," Brandon said unconvincingly. He felt the need to feign normality and forced out a chuckle. "Pretty rough night last night." Buddy laughed knowingly and nodded, shifting his messenger bag on his back.

"Yeah, bro, I hear you. Woke up and didn't know where I was, or who *she* was. What the fuck am I doing with my life?"

Brandon laughed politely. "Hey, could I come in with you? I'm supposed to pick my girlfriend up for brunch but she must be oversleeping or in the shower or something. She's not answering her phone either so I don't know."

Buddy had already unlocked the door, and he stepped aside, waving Brandon in with an exaggeratedly courtly gesture. "Kudos to you, man, for getting up so early. Only reason I'm awake is I had to puke."

Brandon thanked him and moved past him, trying to seem nonchalant and unhurried as he scaled the three flights of stairs to Nasreen's floor. Buddy disappeared down the second-floor hallway without exchanging any more pleasantries; his face had suddenly turned ashen and Brandon imagined he wasn't quite done purging the mistakes of the night before.

Once outside Nasreen's apartment, he knocked. He'd never had to before, so he wasn't sure how audible it was through the solid-seeming door. He knocked harder and harder until he became aware he was making a low keening noise under his breath. Then he stopped and leaned his back against the door, sliding down into a sitting position. He slumped there helplessly, his mind racing through everything yet again, looking for a more coherent course of action he could take.

He tried to remember what he could from movies and TV about breaking in. He reached into his back pocket and was grateful to find his wallet; he didn't remember putting it there. He pulled out a credit card. Feeling skeptical, he tried to wedge it into the crack of the door. It tapped ineffectually against the lock, then got stuck. Hearing footsteps and whistling from the stairs, Brandon panicked, tugging at the card's slippery corner, and dislodged it with some difficulty. He crammed it back in his wallet and stuffed the wallet back into his pocket. Then he scrubbed his hands over his face and tried to look composed.

The footsteps got closer and a short graying man rounded the corner from the landing. He and Brandon spotted each other at the same time. The man hesitated before continuing toward him. Brandon felt himself stiffen even as he tried to act nonchalant. Something about the man made him think he worked there.

"Excuse me, are you here with someone?" the man asked, attempting and failing to sound polite.

Brandon stalled for time answering the question. "Are you the landlord?" he asked.

"Building manager," the man replied. "Now, are you here with someone or not?"

Brandon paused, then shrugged. "Sort of," he said in as flippant a tone as he could muster. "You know Nasreen?"

The man shook his head slowly. "Doesn't ring a bell," he said.

Brandon gestured at the door. "The girl who lives here."

The man shrugged. "Don't know her by that name, but OK."

Brandon continued after a puzzled moment of hesitation. "Well, she let me spend the night, but when I woke up she was already gone. I came out but then remembered I left something in there." He could barely buy his own flimsy story. He hoped it made sense and didn't dig him into a hole he couldn't get out of. "Well, just as the door shut I remembered, and you know how it locks automatically. I've been trying to call her to come let me in but she's not answering."

The man nodded doubtfully. "I can't let you in, of course, just in case," he said.

"I get it," said Brandon. "It wasn't all that important anyway, so I can come get it another time when she's home." He took a breath to help him build up his nerve for the next question. "So were you around when she left? She say anything about where she was going?"

The man seemed to make a series of quick calculations before he answered. "What time did you find her gone?" he asked.

"Only woke up myself a half hour or so ago," Brandon replied. "She could've left any time during the night or this morning."

The man nodded again. "Yep, must have been very early this morning, son." He looked at him with some sympathy. "She called and left me a message, about four a.m."

Brandon could hardly believe what he'd just heard. His heart leapt. "You talked to her?" he cried.

The man looked at him strangely, no doubt wondering why he was so excited about someone talking to a woman he'd just seen — not to mention slept with — the night before.

"Like I said, I got a message from her on my voicemail. I didn't talk to her."

"Right, sorry," Brandon said, trying to curb the shaking in his voice.

"Yeah, so I don't know when you're gonna get your—whatever you left in there. Probably keep trying her phone until she gets back to you."

Brandon couldn't decipher what the man meant. "So she won't be back home anytime soon?"

"Won't be home at all, if you mean here," the man said; evidently the satisfaction of delivering bad news had outweighed his hesitation about sharing a tenant's personal information with a stranger. "Said she needed to break her lease right away; some kind of family emergency and she needed to leave the state. That's why I say you'll have to talk to her about your stuff. The movers'll be here today; that's why I'm here, to let 'em in for her. She's not coming back." He shrugged.

"But what—" Brandon groped for words. "Where is she going? Did she leave you a forwarding address?"

"Nope," the man said. "Maybe she figures she doesn't need to since she's not getting her deposit back. Or she just forgot; she sounded pretty stressed."

"Did she tell you *anything* about where she was going?" Brandon pressed, trying not to sound desperate. "What city, what state?"

It was one question too many, apparently, and the manager clammed up. A note of hostility crept into his voice as he told Brandon he didn't know anything more, he didn't think he should be telling anyone about a tenant's personal business, and he had a lot of things to take care of that morning. Brandon opened his mouth to ask what he meant about not knowing Nasreen by that name, saw the short but sturdy man start to puff himself up as if getting ready to remove him bodily, and hurried away, down the stairs and into the morning sun.

# CHAPTER FIVE

Brandon was nodding off, despite himself, when he saw the moving van pull up to Nasreen's building. He sat up with a jolt, then leaned back again slowly, hoping he'd be less noticeable pressed against the headrest. He watched two bearded men, unkempt hair pasted to their scalps with sweat, get out. One of them raised the back door of the truck and lowered the ramp while the other stood at the entrance to the building with a phone pressed to his ear.

The first man climbed into the van and emerged carrying a number of flattened brown moving boxes bound with hard plastic straps. He tossed the bundle down to the other man and went back into the van to retrieve a second one.

In a minute or two, the door opened and the manager appeared. Holding the door, he spoke to them briefly, then opened it wider to let them in. They walked in past him, each lugging a pack of boxes.

Brandon impatiently waited for them to reappear. He'd been sitting in his car for nearly three hours—ever since he'd left Nasreen's building—and was thirsty, stiff-muscled, and disoriented. In the moment that he'd jerked awake at the arrival of the moving van, he'd once again had a panicked feeling that he was late for class. Once he was fully awake, the sickening recollection of what had really happened was much worse.

At last, the two men reappeared. One of them came out first and flipped the doorstop out to prop the door open, then ducked back in and reappeared carrying one side of a loveseat.

They hauled it up the ramp and disappeared from view again.

While they were in the van, Brandon got out of his car and approached, hoping they hadn't seen that he'd been sitting there already when they pulled up.

As they came out, he smiled and waved. "Hey!" he said. "How's it going?"

The men squinted in the bright sunlight, looking him over. Their clothing was filthy, crusted with baked-in dirt. As he got closer, he could smell rank, days-old sweat emanating from them. "Not bad," one of them said neutrally.

Brandon continued to smile, realizing how forced it must look. "Listen, I was hoping you could do me a favor. That's my girlfriend's stuff you're loading up, and I need to find out where she's going. Could you give me a rough idea?"

The men exchanged glances. Brandon wondered if they were brothers, or father and son. Or maybe it was the uniformity of their clothes, hair, and level of filth that made him think there was a resemblance. The one with some gray in his beard spoke first. "Man, if your girlfriend is leaving town and you don't know where, there's probably a reason for that." Brandon's heart sank.

"I know how it sounds, but it's not like that, really," he assured them, already fumbling for a plausible story. "She's just … kind of flaky and not answering her phone. I'm sure she's gonna call me soon, but I'd … like to surprise her by getting some flowers delivered so they'll be there when she gets there." The men stared at him, unconvinced.

Brandon pulled out his wallet, looked in, found four twenties and some other odd bills. "Hey, I know it's not something you're supposed to do, but if you could just …" he held out the handful of cash wordlessly.

More silence as the men shifted from foot to foot in similar fashion, eyeing the money as if tempted. But the older one shook his head. "No way man, we aren't allowed to give out information like that." They stared at him until he retreated, then went back in the building.

Brandon walked away, past his car and down the street as if heading for a different one. When he figured they were safely inside and focusing on the next piece of furniture to cart out, he doubled back quickly and got into his car, slumping low so he couldn't be seen. He cracked the window so he could hear more clearly, as the two men grunted and cursed their way out the door with another apparently heavy item.

For what felt like an eternity, Brandon hunkered down out of sight in his car, listening to the sounds of the men moving Nasreen's belongings out. He strained to hear any hints of where they were going in their sporadic conversation, but he couldn't make out anything.

Occasionally he raised his head to peer out at them. He saw the younger man bring out a laptop and small printer; instead of putting them in the back, he walked around to the passenger side door and put them in the front of the van. Brandon ducked his head back down, troubled. Maybe they transported electronics up front so they could make sure they weren't jostled in transit, but it seemed strange to him that they wouldn't just package them with plenty of padding and put them in back.

At last he heard the complaining shriek of metal against metal as they put the ramp back into its slot, and the rattle and clang of the back van door being lowered and slammed shut. The moving van's engine rumbled to life and idled briefly. Then Brandon heard the unmistakable sound of the vehicle pulling away and driving down the street.

Brandon straightened, looking around to make sure no one was watching him, and started his car. He pulled out slowly and drove in the direction the van was heading.

It was easy enough to follow the two men through the city streets, sometimes with one or two cars between them. The van made several turns before veering onto the entrance ramp of 99 South. Brandon followed it for a couple miles on the highway, then onto an exit ramp.

They drove through increasingly industrial-looking areas until the moving van reached the open gates of a large building. Brandon cruised by it, slowing but not turning in or stopping, and read the sign on the front: South Transfer Station. It didn't ring a bell for him, so he kept driving until he found an almost deserted parking lot near another building. He pulled in and looked up the name on his phone. A waste disposal facility.

Brandon sat still, mind racing. He tapped frantically on his phone again, locating the nearest ATM, less than ten minutes away. He turned on navigation and followed the mechanical female voice's instructions to it.

Then back to the transfer station. He pulled over a few hundred feet from the entrance and parked, engine running. He wondered if they could've finished unloading in the time it had taken him to drive out to the ATM, withdraw money, and come back.

Brandon's stomach was in a knot. If he went in, he risked being seen by the movers. Wait too long and Nasreen's belongings could be crushed in a compactor, or buried by a ton of garbage, or whatever happened in there. Just as his rising panic pushed him toward entering before it was too late, the moving van emerged from the building and drove quickly toward him. He flung himself down in the seat as far as he could go. When, he sat up a few tense moments later, the van was out of sight.

Brandon pulled out and drove up to the building; a man outside waved him forward and then put his hand out to stop. Brandon rolled down his driver side window and leaned out. The man eyed his small car.

"You got something in the trunk you want to dispose of?" the man asked. "Can't be much—seems like you could've just left it out with the trash."

Brandon smiled and shook his head. "I have a little bit of an unusual request," he said. He opened his door and stepped out. "Can I talk to you for a minute?"

He told the man that his girlfriend had kicked him out, then had all their mutual belongings taken here to be disposed of. He described the moving van he'd seen pulling away from their place. He just wanted to go through and pull out a few sentimental items that she hadn't given him a chance to keep. When he saw the man looked set to give a firm no, Brandon pulled a thick wad of crisp twenties out of his pocket and held them up. "Look, I know I'm putting you in an awkward position. I have five hundred bucks. Could you come up with a way for me to look for my stuff and not get you in trouble?"

The man's eyes narrowed, but then fixed on the money. He glanced around, stepped close, and slipped it out of Brandon's hand. For an elementary school gym teacher it was already a large sum; during the summer months in a year when he'd decided not to get a part-time job and instead stretch his savings to the breaking point, it felt almost ruinous.

At the same time, he was elated; having been dismissed and denied at every turn up until now, he finally felt a little less helpless.

"Get back in your car," the man said. "Follow me and stop when I tell you." Brandon nodded eagerly and drove slowly into a massive open room flooded with natural light from windows high above. Several pickup trucks were parked seemingly at random, their drivers pulling out the contents of the bed and adding them to large piles on the floor. Besides the stacks of garbage everywhere, the facility looked relatively clean and new.

Once inside, the man held up his hand again for him to stop, then walked over to another man standing between two large piles. They exchanged words, and the one who had come in with Brandon gestured over at him. The second man nodded and the first headed back toward Brandon. He leaned in the window.

"You've got ten minutes," he said. "Your stuff's over there." He pointed and Brandon saw the loveseat—the first thing the movers had taken out of Nasreen's apartment—sitting upside down atop a heap of other items.

He drove over to the pile and got out. He felt rushed but at a loss as to where to start. He wasn't familiar enough with Nasreen's

belongings to identify them out of context—
he'd only gone to her place occasionally, and
then it had always been at night after a date—
but he did recognize some of the things he'd
watched the movers load into their van. He
climbed partway up the heap, peered under
the loveseat, then with effort pushed it so it slid
down one side of the pile. He glanced around,
but the men running the place seemed
unconcerned with him for the time being, and
there was plenty of noise coming from the
people unloading and other activities
happening out of Brandon's sight.

He pushed a mattress with bedding still
wrapped around it down the other side of the
hill. He rummaged between boxes and under
lamps and framed art, looking for her laptop or
other devices that might contain information
but could find none. He wondered if the
movers had taken valuables with them.

He began opening boxes. They'd been
stuffed carelessly and chaotically, without
wrapping or cushioning, and many fragile
items were damaged or completely destroyed.

Clearly the men had known their destination. Brandon found plates and glasses that were now little more than shards, small framed pieces of art with shattered glass, tangled necklaces and bracelets thrown indiscriminately in with cosmetics and toiletries, clothes, books, towels, shoes, and more, all crumpled and jumbled together. As he tore open one box after another, Nasreen's scent seemed to gather in the air around him. He picked up a tube of wine-red lipstick, pictured it coating her lips, and felt compelled to slip it into his pocket.

In a box mostly containing office and household supplies, he pushed aside some takeout menus and found a couple postcards. He lifted them out but, aware of time slipping away, folded them and stuffed them in his pocket without reading the backs. Underneath was a sheaf of bills and junk mail. He grabbed a handful, intending to toss them aside and keep digging, but froze instead.

The address was Nasreen's. The name of the recipient was not.

# CHAPTER SIX

He read and reread the name on the envelope. Aisha Khan. He flipped through the entire pile of mail, and the unfamiliar name stared out at him from under every plastic window.

A wave of nausea swept over him without warning. He threw the stack of papers down, then reconsidered and picked up one envelope and crammed it in his pocket.

Then he saw he'd uncovered another framed picture. This one was a photograph. He pulled it out.

The man in the photo stared evenly out from beneath the brim of a military hat—

Marines, Brandon guessed, though he wasn't sure. His face was unsmiling. Brandon stared at the face, wondering if he was a brother? A friend? He didn't look related to Nasreen, but Brandon was realizing they hadn't talked much about her family.

Thinking once again of time running out, he slid the cardboard backing out of the frame and pulled the picture out. Reluctant to fold it, he grabbed an empty folder from the same box and slipped the photo inside.

He rifled through a few other boxes, hurriedly, and recognized with a pang some of the clothing—a dark red V-neck long-sleeve shirt she (and he) had been especially fond of, a sky blue ornamental scarf she sometimes wrapped around her neck when they went out at night. His head swam with unanswered questions about why Nasreen's belongings were now sitting in a pile in this gigantic room full of garbage and noise. And why all her mail was addressed to someone named Aisha.

Unable to settle on anything else to take, and realizing he'd already taken more than ten minutes, Brandon reluctantly returned to his car. He threw the folder on the passenger seat and started the engine.

His stomach wrenched at the thought of leaving the rest of Nasreen's things behind to be destroyed and dumped in a landfill somewhere. At least there hadn't been much that seemed sentimental. He didn't know if that was better or worse, that her belongings about to be compacted into nothing said nothing about her. Not even her name.

He saw the man he'd bribed looking over at him, and so he drove out of the facility.

* * *

Brandon looked at the mail again when he got home. The bill was two months old, which meant Nasreen surely already lived there when it had arrived. He now wished he'd taken more of them to check the dates. He examined the postcards next—one from Istanbul and another from Dubai, postmarked a year before. They were addressed to Nasreen—not Aisha—but to an unfamiliar address in Alexandria, Virginia.

The messages said nothing revealing and were only signed with the initial "T."

Brandon took the photo out of the folder. He searched every detail of the Marine's face, looking for what he wasn't sure. The man was good-looking, but his unsmiling expression was bland and neutral, like every other military portrait Brandon had ever seen. He looked white, with no trace of Pakistani heritage that Brandon could detect—no family resemblance to Nasreen whatsoever.

An internet search of Aisha Khan pulled up many mentions and images, but none of them looked like Nasreen. The address on the postcards was connected to a couple with the last name Johnson. Their names were so common that the search results on them were of no use.

He returned to the photo, tried to think of who might be able to help him identify the man. His own friends had met Nasreen a handful of times; he hadn't met any of hers. She'd taken him to a couple bars that seemed to be her regular haunts. He remembered bartenders greeting her with familiarity.

He was halfway to the first one before realizing it was early afternoon; probably none of the regular staff would be there. Instead he drove back to Nasreen's apartment building. He saw a listing for "OFFICE" on the intercom and pressed the button next to it. A moment of silence, then a hiss and click and "Yeah?"

"Um, hi, I need to speak to someone," he fumbled.

The speaker hissed lightly for a beat or two before it buzzed to let him in. He headed downstairs to the basement. Other than a tangle of bikes and a laundry room, he didn't see anything. He headed back up the steps and rounded the corner to try the main-floor hall. He almost jumped as he saw the building manager peering out a door. The man's expression was guarded as he looked at Brandon, recognizing him from that morning.

"Hi," Brandon said, trying not to sound nervous. "Sorry to bother you again." He suddenly realized he didn't really have a story prepared and began to stammer. "I was wondering, uh, have you seen, uh …" he shoved the photograph at the man. "Have you ever seen this guy around?"

The man looked at him. "Where did you get this?" he said suspiciously.

"It was, uh, in a bag of stuff Nas—my girlfriend left at my place," he said with false nonchalance. "It was a friend of hers, and I was just wondering if you'd seen him in the area, so I could maybe—if he lived near here, I could find him and give him the stuff back." Fully realizing his story didn't make any sense, Brandon held his breath unconsciously.

The man thought about it, and either believed him or didn't feel like fighting it. He took the photo and studied it for a minute or two. "No, I don't think I've seen this guy before." He handed it back to him with a shrug. "I'm not around all the time; I run a few other buildings too, and when I'm here I spend a lot of time in this room. But she didn't have many visitors that I can think of." His eyes held slightly more sympathy than they had the first time Brandon had encountered him.

Brandon took the photo with numb fingers. He felt despair welling up inside him and had to blink back tears. This flimsy lead already felt like a dead end. He thanked the man and went back outside.

At home he lay on his couch and stayed there for hours, staring at the ceiling. He remembered asking to connect with Nasreen on social media and teasing her for being a snob when she told him she didn't participate. He hadn't actually cared that much; as a teacher, he was aware of the potential scrutiny from students, their parents, and the school administration, and kept his time there brief and his own activity neutral. Now he searched every app on his phone both for Nasreen Hassan and for Aisha Khan. Nothing. He searched the web again, going deeper into the results. Not a single result seemed to be about her.

That evening he went out again to the first of Nasreen's two favorite bars, a low-key place called Max's with wood trim and maroon leather barstools. Brandon sat on one until the bartender appeared from the back area, carrying a stack of glass tumblers that he placed carefully on a counter. He was a young man with shaggy brown hair and a short beard and mustache. He saw Brandon and smiled in recognition.

"What can I get for you?" he asked cordially.

Brandon ordered a shot of whiskey and a beer, a combination he ordered when he needed to unwind quickly after a hard day. He downed the shot immediately and followed it with a swig of beer, and by then the bartender had busied himself with other tasks. So Brandon nursed the beer, feeling the effects more immediately than usual. He realized he was drinking on a nearly empty stomach, and it gave him a good excuse to flag the young man down again. "Could I get some pretzels and peanuts?" he called when he caught his eye. The bartender pulled the snacks down from a rack behind the bar and brought them over.

As Brandon was wondering what to say, the man started it for him. "Where's your friend tonight?"

Brandon shrugged, trying to look nonchalant. "I haven't seen her in a couple days," he said. He paused, then said, "Say, did she come here before she brought me?"

"Yeah, she's been a regular for a little while."

"She bring lots of friends here?"

"Uh, not really. She'd usually come alone, or with just one person."

"The same person?"

The bartender thought about it, then shook his head. He hesitated over what he was about to say. "No, just like, uh, casual dates, if I had to guess." He looked sympathetic and added, "But not too often. And she hasn't come with anyone else since she started bringing you."

Brandon's stomach got a hollow feeling, but he nodded. He pulled out the photo of the man in uniform. "Hey, I know it gets busy in here, but did you ever see this guy coming in with her?" He pushed the picture across the polished surface of the bar, and the young man studied it for a few moments, touching the corner of it with his thumb.

At last he shook his head. "No, he doesn't look familiar. You looking for him?"

Brandon shrugged, heartbroken. "Kind of," he said.

"He a friend?"

"Friend of hers, I think," Brandon managed. The bartender nodded as if he understood.

"Don't worry," he said in a comforting tone of voice. "He's cute, but you're cuter. She's gonna stick with you." His eyes locked with Brandon's and his smile deepened. Surprised at the sudden flirtation, Brandon managed only a self-conscious chuckle and thanks. The bartender laughed too, looking pleased at having flustered Brandon, who finished his beer and headed out to the other bar Nasreen seemed to favor.

The staff there was less forthcoming than the first bartender had been, but two servers looked at the photograph. Both said they didn't recognize the man.

Brandon had another drink there and headed home in the dark. He divided his time that night between pacing the house and sitting immobile, reliving the moment she'd disappeared. And going back through their brief history together for signs of trouble, instability, danger, dissatisfaction with him or Seattle or her life. He kept coming back to the thought that she wouldn't do this—he couldn't think of anyone who would hire a moving van to take their belongings to a dump, let alone Nasreen. It didn't make any sense. Anyone who was truly abandoning their life—another thing he couldn't imagine her doing—would just leave everything behind, not bothering to dispose of it.

And they'd take their computer. Brandon couldn't get past that part either.

No. Someone had taken her. Something had happened to her. And the clearing out of her apartment told him that it wasn't a random abduction by a stranger. Something calculated had happened, by someone who wanted to cover their tracks and erase Nasreen's existence.

He wasn't crazy. Was he? His head was foggy from the drinks he'd had on a half-empty stomach. He heated up something in the kitchen and ate it without tasting it. He checked his phone constantly, even though he'd hear it if she texted or called. Nothing but a few texts from friends inviting him places, which he ignored or answered with polite regrets.

Until she'd disappeared, it really hadn't occurred to him that he hadn't met anyone through her. If he *had* thought anything about it, he probably would've assumed that would come later; they'd only been dating a couple months. Now he struggled to think of any connection to her life that could help him find her, or at least find an explanation for why this had happened. The short paths he'd followed had all been complete dead ends. As desperately as his mind searched for new openings, it felt like all trace of Nasreen had been removed from the world.

# CHAPTER SEVEN

Brandon had never been more grateful for the summer break. He couldn't imagine summoning a cheerful expression and the huge amounts of energy needed to rally his hyper, distracted, and/or emotionally needy students. And since he'd decided to take the summer off instead of waiting tables or coaching soccer like he usually did, he didn't have to put on a facade for anyone else either.

At the same time, he felt he was suffering even more because of his free schedule. With no clues leading him to next steps, time seemed to stretch out endless and empty before him.

He thought about going back to the police. Maybe he would get a different officer. But then he tried thinking of what he could tell them. He could give them her address. The building manager would tell them about her moving away. He could tell them about the moving van going to the garbage facility. The employee he'd bribed would probably deny all knowledge of what had happened. He could explain that she wasn't answering her phone, that it seemed to have gone permanently dead. They would assume she'd changed her number to get away from him. He could show them the mail with a different name and her address, and they'd probably arrest him for mail fraud or something.

No, he couldn't go to the police again. He could only hope one of her friends or family members, someone who had known her longer and better than he had, would contact authorities with a more believable story than he had, with more evidence of her existence, with more proof that they were people she loved and not just a nuisance—or worse—that she was trying to escape.

* * *

With nowhere to go and nothing to do, he took to sitting in his car across the street from her apartment building. He'd get fast food and coffee and watch and wait, sometimes flipping through a newspaper or magazine or surfing the news on his phone, for hours. When he needed to use the restroom he'd go home or to another fast food place, then return with an anxious feeling that he might have missed something.

Sometimes he swiped through his few photos of Nasreen on his phone. A selfie of the two of them, the water behind them, sunlight glinting off small waves. A shot of her at a bar, cocktail glass in hand, head thrown back in laughter. And one of her in his bathtub, bubbles up to her shoulders, wet hair slicked back from her face, no makeup, smiling tolerantly at his intrusion.

He carried the lipstick he'd taken from the pile of her belongings, the postcards, and the photo of the mystery man with him at all times. He had no other mementos from their time together, so he clung to them like talismans. Even though he hadn't known of the man's existence during the time he'd spent with Nasreen, and it hadn't led him any closer to finding out what had happened to her, the photo still felt important. He'd sometimes study the implacable expression and handsome features of the man as if a message might be hidden there.

Hardly anyone seemed to notice him sitting in his car, and when it got dark it was even easier to escape the eyes of the neighbors. More and more often he stayed all night, dozing on and off; otherwise he'd go home and sleep fitfully, or go and wander the street where she'd disappeared, reliving the moment and looking for faces or vehicles that resembled her presumed captors or their car.

He sometimes went home to shower, shave, and put on new clothes, daily at first, then every two or three days.

Two weeks went by like this. Brandon deflected friends' communications and invitations in a way he hoped wouldn't cause concern. Sometimes he wondered what his life would look like in a month when school started. Would he have given up his vigil and go back to teaching as if this whole summer had never happened? If Nasreen never reappeared in his life, would he find someone else? Would he ever get over this?

One evening, as the sun was setting, an emptiness gripped him. The universe seemed a cold and meaningless place. He pressed his hands to his face but no tears came. Instead, a flood of images: her hand in his, her eyes confiding, seemingly adoring as they glanced over at him. Nasreen gripping a wide cappuccino mug with both hands and talking passionately about an issue, the familiar little furrow appearing between her eyebrows. Nasreen swaying to live music, pressed into him. Nasreen above him in the dim light of his bedroom lamp, her skin glistening as she rose and fell.

Brandon took his hands away from his face and got out of his car, needing to stretch his muscles and get some fresh air. He gulped it in, his chest feeling tight and constricted, his stomach roiling.

A taxi rolled up to Nasreen's apartment building, and Brandon instinctively ducked behind his car. He always tried to remain as inconspicuous as possible in the hopes that none of her neighbors would find his presence suspicious and call the cops on him.

The cab idled; Brandon guessed the passenger was paying their fare. Soon a tall, broad-shouldered man unfolded himself from the back of the cab. The trunk popped open and he lifted out a large military-style duffel bag and heaved it onto his shoulder.

The driver had gotten out to help, but seeing that the man had already grabbed his belongings, he merely shut the trunk and got back in. The man walked toward Nasreen's building and the taxi drove away.

As Brandon watched from behind his car, the man checked the building directory and pressed a button to buzz in. He waited, then tried a few more times, apparently unsuccessful. He craned his neck and looked up at the building. Brandon saw him pull out a phone and hold it to his ear. Again, he seemed to be unsuccessful in getting through to whomever he expected to reach. He shifted his feet absently, turning in a slow circle, as he redialed and waited again, and the soft glow of a streetlight that had only recently come on caught his features and showed them clearly to Brandon for the first time.

Brandon froze. It was the man in the photo.

# CHAPTER EIGHT

It had taken Brandon a moment to recognize him without the uniform and hat set low on his forehead. He had short-cropped dark hair and was in civilian clothes. The man tried the buzzer one more time, then let his bag drop to the ground by his feet. He appeared to be looking something up on his phone. Brandon hesitated. He was afraid if he approached him the wrong way, he might lose the last possible thread to Nasreen's existence.

The man touched his smartphone screen one more time, then slipped the device in his pocket and stood, arms folded, next to his bag, looking around the street. Whether he was worried or not Brandon couldn't tell from his hiding place.

Although the man was physically imposing—at least as tall as Brandon and more muscled—he didn't look agitated or threatening. Brandon steeled himself and started across the street.

"Hi," he called when he got halfway, and waved. The man turned to look at him. It was disorienting for Brandon to see the features he'd studied countless times on a living person. The man was even more handsome in real life, and his eyes and mouth had friendly crinkles around them that hadn't showed in his serious military portrait. A hint of a smile seemed to play on his lips. At the same time, his body had a certain coiled readiness—relaxed but prepared for action—and his height and muscles were even more imposing up close. Brandon's stomach flipped nervously as he got closer.

"Um, hi," he said again, starting to hold his hand out, then hesitating. "I—are you looking for Nasreen Hassan?"

The man gave him a measured look. "Why do you ask?" His voice was as calm as his body language and expression. If he was worried or angry, he didn't show it.

"I, um, I'm looking for her too. She's been gone for, like, a couple weeks. I'm her friend." He did hold his hand out at that point. "Brandon. Stewart."

The other man sized him up for a beat or two longer, then extended his own hand and shook Brandon's. His grip was firm and his hand dry. Brandon was pretty sure his was clammy.

"Troy Weathers," the man said. "You haven't seen her for a couple of weeks? Have you heard from her?"

Brandon shook his head. He told himself to control his terror so he wouldn't seem unbalanced. "I haven't been able to reach her since—well, it's kind of a strange story." He shifted from foot to foot, glanced at the building, thought of Nasreen's probably still empty apartment. "Listen, can I buy you a drink and tell you about it? My car's right over there."

Troy thought about it. "Well, I just ordered a ride, but—" he looked Brandon over again "—I can cancel it." Without another word he hoisted his duffel bag again and followed Brandon to his car.

Brandon popped the trunk and got in the driver's seat. He caught sight of the postcards and Troy's photo on the passenger seat and hurriedly stuffed them into the glove compartment. His heart was pounding madly. He felt like he was coaxing a strange animal to approach him and didn't want to make any sudden moves that would send it bounding away from him, never to be seen again. He tried to sit calmly and not crane his neck to make sure Troy was really coming.

Then he felt a slight movement as the heavy bag was heaved into his trunk and his whole body flooded with relief. The trunk slammed and Troy approached the passenger side.

When he tried to open the door and it was locked, Brandon hastily hit the unlock button on his door to let him in. At last the man entered his car and sat down, looking for the release to move the seat back. Of course, Brandon thought glumly, the last person who'd sat there was Nasreen with her five-five frame. This guy was easily six-three; at least two inches taller than Brandon.

He started the engine and pulled away. In his current state he struggled to remember where any bar was, and could only come up with Max's.

The car ride was silent at first; he hadn't been playing the radio at all these past few weeks, so music didn't come on when the car started. He didn't want to start talking about what had happened while he was driving; it would be too strange as the first thing Troy heard from him. He felt the need to establish some sense of normality first.

Finally he cleared his throat slightly. "So, you military?" he asked, trying to sound conversational.

"Yeah," Troy said, matching his blandly pleasant tone. "I guess my bag gave me away, huh?"

"Yeah," Brandon fibbed with a chuckle. "Did you just come back from a trip or something?" He felt stupid saying it, but he was suddenly unsure if "tour of duty" was the right phrase.

"Yeah, I've actually just left the Marines," Troy said.

"Oh, wow!"

"Just got back from my last assignment and ready to enter civilian life, I guess." Troy seemed to reflect on that for a few moments. "How about you? What do you do?"

"Teacher," Brandon said. "Well," he added with a tone of self-deprecation, "gym teacher. Elementary school."

"That's cool."

"It's OK, I guess."

They lapsed into silence again, but Brandon felt better, like he'd shown he could have a regular conversation before trying to take Troy down the rabbit hole with him. In a way it would feel more difficult now that he'd established a casual tone, but it would be hard either way.

He found a parking spot on the street a half-block past Max's. Troy pleasantly asked him to pop the trunk so he could get his duffel; he lifted it easily despite its obvious weight. Brandon felt he hadn't won the man's trust if he didn't want to leave his things in the car, but he was careful not to express any hesitation or objection. The two of them walked back the other way toward the bar. "You been here before?" Brandon asked Troy as he held the door for him.

"No, actually this is my first time in Seattle," Troy said. There was a "Seat yourself" sign by the unattended hostess station, so Brandon led the way to a booth near the back. "I was overseas for about a year, and when I wasn't stationed somewhere I was mainly on the East Coast."

Brandon nodded as Troy wedged his bag into the corner of the booth and the men sat down facing each other. "So where do you know Nasreen from?" he asked.

"You mean where I met her?"

"Sure."

"That was in D.C., about three, maybe four years ago." Troy stopped for a second. "No, yeah, four years. Being away kind of messed up my sense of time." He leaned forward, and though his voice remained even, Brandon could finally see some cracks in his calm exterior; a tenseness to his neck, a set to his jaw as if he was clenching his teeth a little. He was ready to abandon the small talk. "So what's this strange story you wanted to tell me?"

Just then the waitress appeared and took their drink order. Troy sat back, smiling charmingly at her as if he wasn't at all tense. Brandon could see the woman melt a little as she met Troy's eyes. Brandon looked away and saw that the bartender who had flirted with him a few weeks before was behind the bar, looking over at them with unabashed curiosity. Brandon nodded and smiled at him and it was returned.

"Well, so, we were … hanging out one night, about two weeks ago," Brandon began, once the waitress had left and Troy once again looked at him with questioning eyes. He realized he still wasn't sure what the man's relationship was to Nasreen. Had they been dating? Had it been serious? Were they *still* dating as far as Troy was concerned? If so, he didn't want to say too much about his own feelings for Nasreen and potentially turn the focus on the wrong thing. They could sort that out later; right now Troy was possibly the last lifeline to finding out where Nasreen had gone.

While he hesitated, the waitress came back with their drinks. Brandon waited until she was probably out of earshot, then started his story again.

He told of the last minutes before losing Nasreen, describing the scene of her standing by the men's car as well as he could. He skimmed over how the police had treated him, just saying they had told him to come back when more time had passed. He talked about the building manager's voicemail from

Nasreen and the movers, about following the moving van to the waste disposal site.

He skipped the part where he bribed the dump officials and took the framed photo of Troy from Nasreen's discarded belongings. Even though it was precisely what led him to recognize the man, it would just sound too extreme, he thought. That precluded him from talking about the mail in the name Aisha Khan. Instead he ended with her phone being dead or turned off, no one showing up at the apartment building until Troy, and no calls or emails from her.

Troy listened. Other than a word here and there to show he was interested, he didn't interrupt Brandon as the flood of words poured out of him. The relief of telling someone after weeks of isolation and near silence soon overcame his fear of scaring the man off.

He came up for air and took a shaky breath. "Do you think I'm making a big deal out of nothing?" he asked at last. "Does it all sound as crazy as I think it does? I haven't talked to anyone about it, so I don't know anymore."

Troy's face was still unreadable, so Brandon waited tensely for him to speak.

"No, I don't think it's nothing," he said slowly.

Brandon didn't try to conceal his relief. "So do you think you could help me look for her? Do you know her family or other friends? We've only been … friends for a couple months, so I didn't know where else to look. Maybe since you've known her longer, you could help me ask around, see if anyone has heard from her. Maybe …" his voice cracked and he hesitated until he could speak normally. "I just really want to know she's OK."

Troy nodded contemplatively. He drained his drink. "Look, man," he said finally, "you've been really helpful. I can't thank you enough for all the time you spent looking for her and for telling me everything. It sounds like you and Nasreen are … very good friends." The slight hesitation signaled to Brandon that Troy probably suspected they were more than that.

"And I promise you, I'm going to try and find her. I *will* find her. But I think it's better if I just do it on my own, you know? But I'll tell Nasreen what a great friend you were, and I'm sure she'll get in touch with you down the road when she can."

Brandon's stomach dropped. "No, come on," he said desperately. "I really *want* to help. I'm sure there's something I can do to make it easier. If we work together, I bet we can …" He trailed off as Troy stood up, dropping a twenty-dollar bill on the table between them. The man shouldered his duffel bag.

"Really, it's not necessary," Troy said, not unkindly. "I appreciate all your help already, but I can take it from here." He reached out his hand for Brandon to shake it but got only a panicked look in return. He lowered his arm. "Take care, OK? You seem like a good guy." With that, he headed out the bar.

# CHAPTER NINE

Brandon froze in horror, seeing his last connection to Nasreen disappearing into thin air. Then his paralysis broke and he jumped up, leaving the money on the table and pushing past the waitress, feeling her and the bartender's curious eyes on him as he rushed out.

He burst onto the street with a sense of déjà vu from the night Nasreen had disappeared. He stared wildly around him, people blurring into a faceless throng. But then he spotted a tall figure with a large bag walking away and ran after him.

He caught up with Troy by the entrance to a narrow alley and grabbed his arm. The man whirled around, looking ready to fight, and Brandon quickly released him and raised his hands. "It's OK, it's OK," he said. "I just wanna talk to you." He jerked his head toward the alley, imploring Troy with his eyes.

The man paused, then sighed and shrugged and stepped out of the busy street into the alley. He set his duffel down, leaned against one of the buildings that formed the alley walls, and folded his arms. "What do you want?" he asked Brandon.

Brandon felt himself crumbling. He clenched his fists and looked down for a moment, trying to regain control, but his whole body was trembling. He looked up again. "She was … getting to be a really big part of my life," he said. "I know I haven't known her as long as you, but you must know how … amazing she is. I bet she was important to you right away, when you didn't know her for very long. Right?"

Troy cocked his head, possibly in assent.

"Well, when she … left," Brandon continued, awkward and desperate, "and when her phone didn't pick up, and she wouldn't email, it hit me that I didn't have any other connections to her. I'd never met any of her friends, I didn't know her parents or where they lived—" he stopped. He couldn't tell if he was getting through at all. Brandon felt as if he might collapse. He searched Troy's eyes for a sign of compassion.

"Please," he said quietly. "If you leave, I don't have anything, anyone, any way to ever reach Nasreen." He hesitated. "I don't know who you are. I—I don't understand any of this. Just let me help you and I promise I won't get in the way if …" He lowered his head to try and hide the tears welling up.

He felt a hand on his shoulder and looked up. Troy's face finally registered sympathy, maybe pity, he couldn't tell. All Brandon cared about was that he hadn't walked away again.

* * *

He composed himself as the two returned to his car, and Brandon drove home. Troy had planned to stay at Nasreen's when he'd arrived in Seattle, so Brandon invited him to stay in his second bedroom, which was set up as his office but also had a pullout sofa bed.

Brandon ordered pizza when they got home and cracked open beers. Troy steered the conversation toward innocuous topics, and Brandon followed his lead. He was full of questions, but he only asked what Troy thought they should do next. "I'll make some calls in the morning" was the only response, so he left it at that.

He couldn't stop stealing glances at Troy, the face in the photograph brought to life, and feeling awash with good luck to have a new thread connecting him to Nasreen. And the man's quiet air of confidence made him feel as if there was hope of finding her again.

* * *

Brandon spent the night in his own bed for a change instead of his car, and he slept better than he had since Nasreen's disappearance. But he awoke with a jolt from a dream that Troy had disappeared as inexplicably as he'd appeared.

He staggered out of bed and into the hallway, disoriented but with a lingering feeling of dread from his nightmare. He opened the door of the guest room and saw the sofa bed open, sheets twisted, empty. His stomach dropped and he raced down the short hallway to the living room and kitchen. Also empty. He turned, still dazed, and went back down to where the bathroom was, at the end of the hall. He turned the doorknob, or tried to, and realized it was locked.

As his head began to clear, he heard movement in the bathroom. He regained just enough clarity to feel embarrassed at his dream-induced panic when the door opened, warm steam seeping out at him. Troy stood in the doorway, a towel around his waist and a quizzical look on his face. "I was just finishing up," he said. "Hope it was OK to use your shower."

"Yeah, of course, sorry," Brandon said, completely lucid and mortified. "I, uh, just wondered if you'd like any coffee."

"Yeah, that'd be great," Troy said, though his mouth twitched as if trying to stifle an amused smile. "Sorry, I didn't mean to—"

"Oh yeah, no, totally," Brandon said, backing away, trying not to seem as if he was staring at Troy's muscled chest and lean waist. "Help yourself to whatever. Do you have a change of clothes? I've got plenty of everything if, you know, you need ..." He trailed off, feeling self-conscious in only T-shirt and briefs, with bleary eyes and rumpled hair.

As soon as Troy closed the door, Brandon ducked into his room and threw on some sweatpants, then went to make coffee so his excuse wasn't quite so obviously fabricated. He felt flustered for some reason, even though he'd seen plenty of half-dressed men in locker rooms in his time. Of course not many had a physique like Troy's. Brandon's stomach dropped, hollow and achy. Suddenly comparing himself to Troy, it seemed ludicrous that he, a stupid, sheltered, awkward gym teacher, could have ever meant anything to Nasreen when she had someone like *him* in her life.

He heard the bathroom door open and close, then the guest bedroom's. He had a pot going and was rooting around for breakfast foods that weren't expired when Troy emerged in clean clothes, freshly shaven, hair still damp. Brandon poured a cup of coffee and handed it to him, smiling to hide his roiling emotions. Troy took it and grinned back, the skin on either side of his mouth crinkling into laugh lines.

After a breakfast of granola bars—the eggs, milk and bread all seemed suspect, and Brandon ended up throwing them away—Troy returned to the guest room to make calls.

"I'll let you know if I find out something," he said, pre-empting questions from Brandon. "These are kind of sensitive contacts from Nasreen's work. I shouldn't say much about them unless I need to."

Brandon didn't press it. Nasreen had told him she was a contract project manager, and he'd never asked her for more details, not even really knowing what project managers did. She didn't talk about it much so he assumed it wasn't a very interesting job. They'd always had other things on their minds anyway.

So Brandon waited in the living room, drinking coffee and browsing mindlessly on his phone. He heard talking in the next room but couldn't make out any of the words.

When Troy came out, he looked considerably more serious. "I've got someone who'll talk to us, but he wouldn't do it on the phone," he said.

Brandon sprang up, his heart pounding. "Who is it? When can we meet him?"

"We have to go to Washington."

"But where—" Brandon stopped. "You mean D.C.?"

Troy nodded.

"Oh," Brandon said. He thought about it, about his depleted finances since he'd bribed the garbage facility employee and eaten takeout food for two weeks. But he still had his credit card, and no obligations for another month. "OK, should we book a flight?" He picked up his phone again.

But Troy was already looking on his. "I've got this," he told Brandon.

"I want to come too," Brandon said quickly.

"I know," Troy said. "I mean I've got *our* tickets."

"Oh," Brandon said again, feeling embarrassed but grateful. "Thanks."

# CHAPTER TEN

Troy found seats on a flight leaving that afternoon. Even though he had hours to prepare, Brandon hurried to shower and change. He stuffed a few changes of clothes into a backpack and threw in a book of short stories Nasreen had gotten him that he'd been too occupied with her to ever read beyond the first few pages.

He offered Troy another backpack that was smaller and more manageable than his duffel bag. He was gratified when it was accepted, knowing Troy trusted him enough to leave the rest of his belongings at his house.

In a few hours they were in Brandon's car on the way to the airport. Brandon was dazed with the sudden change from the solitude and monotony of the past weeks. He stuck close to Troy through the check-in and boarding process.

Seated by himself, he suddenly had too much time to think. Meeting Troy had brought more questions than answers.

For one, he couldn't discern Troy's relationship with Nasreen. He doubted his own sincerity in swearing he wouldn't come between them if they were together. He'd felt like he'd meant it at the time, but it had been an impulsive promise born of desperation, and now he wasn't sure. Maybe he didn't have a chance anyway; they might have something he couldn't compete with. But if so, why had she gotten involved with him?

Maybe she hadn't meant to fall for anyone and had been taken by surprise. He'd never cheated, never contemplated being with anyone else when he was dating someone, but he'd never had a long-term, long-distance relationship. He had no idea of the challenges that must pose. The loneliness alone would be difficult.

He felt guilty thinking that he might have unknowingly caused a rift in someone else's relationship. Then again, he hadn't detected much of a reaction from Troy on finding out about Brandon, so maybe he was imagining a relationship that didn't even exist. But he found Troy so inscrutable; he could be hiding how he really felt.

As confusing as it all was, now that there seemed to be some chance of finding Nasreen again, he couldn't help feeling a flicker of hopefulness. But he also needed Troy to be an ally, so he didn't want to appear to pose a threat to whatever it was Troy had—or thought he had—with Nasreen.

He tried to stop his thoughts going in circles by reading his book, but he found himself rereading paragraphs without being able to absorb their meaning. Eventually he fell into a fitful sleep and woke up disoriented as the plane touched down with a jerk. The sky was dark and the tarmac lights were illuminated.

Troy was waiting for him at the gate, and Brandon felt an odd flood of relief to see him. Troy jerked his head and led the way.

They followed signs for ground transportation. Troy caught sight of a man in a suit, holding up a tablet with his name on the screen. He tapped Brandon's arm and they followed the man to a shiny black car. The air outside was hot and thick and close. They climbed in the back seat, declining the driver's offer to put their backpacks in the trunk.

Brandon had only been to D.C. once, years before. He gazed out the window as they were driven down unfamiliar highways and then unfamiliar streets.

"Can you tell me who we're going to see?" he asked. Troy put his finger to his lips and mimicked writing with an invisible pen on the palm of his left hand.

Brandon rooted around in the pockets of his backpack and found a pen and a crumpled envelope. He passed them over to Troy, who scribbled briefly and passed them back.

Brandon glanced in the rearview mirror to see if the driver was watching them in it, but the man seemed intent on driving, so he looked down at the envelope and studied Troy's scrawled note with help from a streetlight they were passing. "Ex FBI. N's mentor. Might know her assnmt." Brandon stared at the words for what felt like a long time. Finally he wrote "What's N's job," then slid the envelope across the seat. Troy picked it up, glanced down, then up at Brandon. He couldn't see the man's expression in the dark.

Finally Troy reached over and plucked the pen from Brandon's fingers. He scratched something on the envelope and handed both back to Brandon.

Brandon looked at the envelope and would have felt shocked, except so much had happened over the past few weeks that his ability to be surprised had been dulled.

Troy hadn't written anything new. He'd merely circled and underlined "FBI" where he'd previously written it.

# CHAPTER ELEVEN

Brandon sat back against the leather seat and stared out the window again. He felt a little more foolish with every revelation about Nasreen. It seemed he'd been blind to every important detail about her life—she'd apparently hidden a lot from him.

At last the car turned into a long driveway and pulled up to a white house with pillars on either side of double front doors. The driver opened Brandon's door.

He stood on the driveway clutching his backpack. The driver said goodnight and got back in the car, not seeming to expect payment or tip. The two men followed the pristine white walkway up to the front porch, and Troy rang the bell.

The door opened and a man stood in the entryway. He had gray thinning hair, a short-sleeve polo shirt and khaki shorts. A pair of reading glasses perched on his forehead. He smiled. "Troy!" he said. "Good to see you, sir!" He stepped out and gave the taller man a hug, then nodded at Brandon and waved them both in. Troy introduced Brandon.

"Michael Dupont," the man said. They shook. "Good to meet you. Friend of Troy's?"

Troy answered before Brandon could decide what to say. "Sort of. Friend of Nasreen's."

"Even better—no offense, Troy," the man said with a light chuckle. "Come on in and let's get you some drinks. How was your trip?"

With Troy and Michael making small talk, the three passed through a polished living room and modern kitchen to a den with well-worn furniture and a big TV. Michael returned to the kitchen and emerged wheeling a silver cart. "Have you ever had aquavit?" he asked Brandon, who shook his head. "Oh, you have to try it then."

He fixed drinks with a practiced hand. Brandon shifted impatiently, perched on the edge of a soft couch cushion, as the other two men continued to chat about people and events he knew nothing about. He clutched his drink and took small frequent sips. It was an effort not to grimace each time the unfamiliar, weirdly astringent liquid hit his tongue, but he had nothing else to do with his nervous energy.

After a few minutes, the day of travel began to catch up to him, and he slowly relaxed into the sofa. Michael turned and smiled warmly at him. "So what do you do, Brandon?" he asked.

Whether it was the cozy room or the man's friendly air, Brandon felt more at ease than he had in weeks. He told Michael about his school, his students, his occasional summer soccer coaching gigs. He felt gratified at how interested both men seemed.

"And how do you know Nasreen?" Michael asked.

Brandon hesitated. There was so much he hadn't said to Troy. But Michael's kind eyes somehow dissipated his fear. "We met in Seattle," he started. "A few months ago." As he talked, he found himself smiling about his memories of her for the first time since her disappearance. He'd run into her, literally, in a park while chasing a soccer ball kicked wildly by one of his friends, and she'd laughed while he helped her to her feet, stammering and apologizing profusely. Although he hadn't made an attempt to flirt or get her number, he felt a pang as he watched her walk away. Then, as if by magic, they'd seen each other at a bar a few days later. He approached her with the excuse of buying her an apology drink. That night they talked for hours, and he did get her number at the end.

He felt himself rambling about their relationship, but Michael and Troy seemed to be listening sympathetically. He got to the part Troy had already heard, about the night everything had changed, and related all that had happened afterward, including some things he'd held back, like finding his photo and the mail addressed to another name. He glanced at Troy several times to see how he felt about the new parts of his story, but he seemed unfazed and even smiled encouragingly, so Brandon kept going.

Michael pressed him persistently but gently for details and he did his best to describe everything he remembered. When he could offer nothing more, Michael stood. "You done with your drink?"

Brandon looked down at the forgotten glass in his hand and saw that he'd drunk it all; there was now only a bit of water where the ice cubes had started to melt. Michael reached for it. "You want another?"

Brandon hesitated before shaking his head. The buzz was pleasant but surprisingly strong after one drink; the light from the lamp next to him had a fuzzy quality, and the room seemed to move slightly when he looked around. Michael took the glass and thanked him in a

cordial tone. He held it up to the light—
Brandon realized he was using a cloth napkin
and holding it by one edge—and then set it
carefully aside.

"Michael, can you tell us anything about
what she was doing out in Washington?" Troy
said, his voice at last revealing a hint of
impatience.

Michael returned to his seat. "We had
dinner a couple nights before she left. She told
me she'd be working out of the Seattle field
office. She didn't say how long she'd be gone
but did say she might be going undercover,
depending on how the case went."

"Do you know anything about the case?"
Troy pressed. Brandon, starting to feel drowsy
and unfocused, was glad of his persistence.
Their voices had a muffled, distant sound in
Brandon's ears.

"Not really. Something to do with a
possible human trafficking ring. And she
mentioned connections to Ukraine. She didn't
tell me much about her work once I retired. I
remember thinking it was unusual she shared

even that much. But you know if it's Nasreen on the case, it's serious. They wouldn't waste her on something minor."

Troy's eyes were distant. His usually half-smiling mouth was set tensely.

"What do you think about what happened that night she disappeared?" he asked. "And the stuff with the movers?"

Michael fixed more drinks for him and Troy, frowning down at the glasses. Then he looked up. "I can see two possibilities. One is that she's gone undercover, like she said she might." He paused. "The other is—that she's been taken by someone who found out what she was doing."

"It seems like she was already undercover, judging from the fake name," Troy said. "If she was planning on ditching that identity that night, why would she be out with him"—he jerked his head toward Brandon, who was too preoccupied with trying to stay alert to react—"and let him see her getting into that car?"

"It doesn't add up," Michael agreed. He took a sip and sighed.

* * *

Brandon felt a hand on his shoulder, shaking him, and heard his name. He opened his eyes with effort to see Troy leaning over him. "It's time to go."

Brandon straightened up and looked around. He was still on the couch in Michael's den. There was a sports talk show on TV and Michael was gone.

Before Brandon could get his mouth working enough to ask where he was, Michael came back in from another room, holding a notepad. He started to speak, but stopped when he saw that Brandon was awake. Instead, he tore off a couple sheets of paper and offered them to Troy.  "Here are some leads you can follow up on," he said.

Troy reached for the notes, but Michael held them away. "I know I don't need to tell you this, but you didn't get any of this from me and we never spoke about it."

Troy assented quickly and was given the papers.

"If you want my advice," said Michael, "I think you should talk to the Seattle field office. Honestly it might be easier to get someone to listen to you out there than trying to wade through the bureaucratic jungle here. Depending on how much Nasreen involved them, they might not even know anything about what she's working on, but they could liaise with D.C. to get a fuller picture and, if there's cause for concern, mobilize to help her."

"I appreciate that," said Troy, "but I don't know how seriously they'd take a tip from us. And they wouldn't let us in on anything they found out even if they did."

Michael shook his head, resigned. "Just find her then, OK?"

Troy asked if Brandon needed help getting up. He shook his head apologetically, struggled to his feet, and followed Troy as Michael escorted them back through the house to the front door. They shook hands and stepped outside, where another car was waiting for them.

"I'm sorry, I don't know what happened," Brandon said as the car pulled out of the long drive. Troy didn't reply, but he asked the driver to pull into a shopping center.

"You stay here," he said to Brandon. "I'll grab us something to eat."

Brandon didn't object. His limbs felt leaden anyway. He leaned his head against the back of the seat, and the cold leather against his neck woke him up a little more. He stared at the roof, wondering how one drink could affect him so strongly. He checked his phone; it was after midnight, but that was only nine o'clock Seattle time.

Troy returned, and gave the driver directions to take them to a motel, a fifteen-minute journey. Brandon shouldered his backpack as the car pulled away from the entrance.

Troy once again took charge, checking them in. Brandon hardly noticed; he was consumed by a dawning realization.

He kept quiet until they were inside the room. While Troy went around turning on lights and putting his backpack and groceries down, Brandon hung back near the door.

Troy noticed that he hadn't moved. "What's up?" he said.

# CHAPTER TWELVE

Brandon's breathing was uneven, a combination of fear and rage rising in him. "Have I been drugged?" he asked. "Did you and Michael fucking put something in my drink?" His trembling hand touched the doorknob behind him, preparing for an escape if Troy came at him.

But Troy stayed where he was, his expression inscrutable as ever. "*I* didn't. But I'm pretty sure Michael did. And he's probably gonna run your fingerprints from the glass you used."

Brandon was frozen. "What the fuck? Why did he—if you knew—why didn't you do anything about it?"

Troy shrugged. "I figured he was trying to get your guard down so he could get more out of you." He started taking wrapped sandwiches and sodas out of a plastic bag. "He didn't tell me he was doing it, but when you started acting so out of it, I guessed. By then it was too late—and I figured it wouldn't be such a bad thing to hear what you had to say." He looked up. "Turns out you did tell him some things you didn't tell me before, so …"

"I can't fucking believe this," Brandon said, almost to himself. "Why did I think I could trust you?"

Troy set a bag of chips on the bedside table that separated the double beds in the room. He folded his arms, a now-familiar posture. "It was shitty of him, but this is the kind of person we'll be dealing with," he said. "If you want to leave, I totally get it. I'll even pay for your ticket back."

Brandon breathed heavily, his mind racing, even more angered—and unexpectedly hurt—by Troy's seeming lack of surprise or remorse for what had happened to him. He'd felt that he had an ally in his search for Nasreen—now he didn't know.

But he couldn't bring himself to leave. To go back to his empty, dead-end existence with no hope and no connection to her was inconceivable.

He had no choice. At least now he knew he couldn't trust anyone; he'd just have to keep his guard up. He let go of the door handle and dropped his backpack on the floor.

* * *

They sat on their beds eating sandwiches, the TV playing a procedural crime show in the background, as Troy looked over the notes Michael had given them. He'd called several old friends to ask what they knew about human trafficking operations with ties to Ukraine. One name had come up with two sources: Diavol. He was rumored to head up a criminal enterprise mainly based in D.C. but with activity on the West Coast as well. Several small drug and prostitution busts had surfaced the name, but none of Michael's friends knew his full name or real identity.

"So maybe Nasreen went out there to bust a bigger ring, and they found out?" Brandon said tentatively. His silent fuming had gradually given way to curiosity as Troy talked.

Troy closed his eyes and rubbed his forehead. "I don't know," he said. "Grabbing an FBI agent off the street—it seems pretty ballsy." He opened his eyes and Brandon for the first time thought he saw fear in them. "If they did take her, I—" He broke off and shook his head. "We have to think she's alive."

Brandon felt sick. His mind had been circling the possibility of the specter Troy had just raised, but he'd managed to stay in denial. Now, horrifying images flashed unbidden into his mind—Nasreen's body, broken and lifeless.

"You can't think about that," Troy said firmly, as if reading his thoughts. "You're no good to her *or* me if you lose hope." The flicker of visible fear was gone, and he once again radiated strength and calm. "Hear me? We don't know enough to assume anything yet."

Brandon stared at him, dazed. "OK," he said, his voice sounding far away in his own ears.

* * *

The next day Troy rented a car and they drove into D.C., to the neighborhood informally known as Little Odessa. When he'd first heard the name, Brandon couldn't help but visualize streets full of pushcart vendors and Old World charm, but when they actually got there, Little Odessa looked much like other residential areas of Washington; blocks lined with brick row houses, peppered by occasional restaurants, bars, and corner markets.

Gentrification and homogenization had made their mark. Brandon and Troy passed at least two modern-looking wine bars, an upscale vintage clothing store, a pastry shop displaying tiny cakes with colorful fondant and intricate designs. A few more lived-in establishments advertised foods like borsch and pierogi, signs of the cultural heritage that had given the neighborhood its name. The passersby seemed to be a mix—perhaps a slightly higher than usual ratio of people with distinctively Eastern European features, but if Brandon hadn't been looking for it, he may not have noticed.

Michael had managed to obtain the names of a few businesses linked in some way to Diavol's activities or associates. Troy led the way to the first one on his list.

The man who looked up as the bell above the door tinkled was more like what Brandon had imagined he would see in the neighborhood. Ancient, stoop-shouldered, with a fringe of white hair and a flour-coated apron over his button-down shirt, he shuffled toward them behind the counter, which displayed rustic loaves of bread and trays of small salt-covered bread rolls. "Can I help you?" he said in a thickly accented voice.

Troy took the lead, leaning on the counter so he could speak in a low voice and be heard.

"Yes, we need your help. We're looking for someone." The man stared at him. "We're trying to find a man called Diavol. You know anything about him?"

At the mention of the name, the old man flinched, but he recovered quickly, busying himself with straightening a plateful of rolls.

"No, no," he said softly as he did so, "don't know anyone like that." He started to turn away, but Troy stopped him with a gentle hand on his arm. The man flinched again but stayed by the counter.

"Hold on," said Troy. He pulled out his wallet and slipped some twenties out, folding them and holding his hand out to the man. The man looked tempted but shook his head after some hesitation.

"Please, I know nothing," he said, a hint of pleading in his voice. He tried moving away again, and this time Troy let him go.

"He knew something all right," he muttered to Brandon as they walked out. At the next place they tried, a cafe serving tea and unfamiliar pastries, they got a similar reaction from the younger man working the counter there. Brandon and Troy stayed to eat a snack and drink some strong, sweet, creamy tea, hoping the man would loosen up if given time. But he avoided their table except to deliver their order and then the check.

The restaurant they entered next was shabby but clean, with an adjoining bar, and no one manning either at this early hour. The aroma of cooking potatoes, onions, and other savory foods hung in the air, and they could hear pots and pans clanging distantly behind a closed door at the back. Troy shrugged at Brandon and led the way to the bar, where they each took a stool and waited.

In a few minutes, a woman emerged from the back, wiping her hands on a kitchen towel. Her white hair was pulled back in a tight bun but wisps had come loose and her face looked damp with perspiration. She approached them unsmiling. "I get you drink?" she said in a gravelly voice.

"Beer, please," said Troy, and Brandon echoed his request.

She filled glasses from a tap, not bothering to ask them what kind they'd like, and set them on the counter. "Three dollar each," she said.

"I got both," Brandon said and handed her a ten. She dropped some ones on the counter and started to turn away. "Keep it," he added, and she turned back to scoop up the bills, nodding her thanks.

Troy jumped in before she could turn away again. "We're looking for Diavol; do you know where he is?" he asked.

There was no flinch this time, just a tired look of recognition. "Diavol," she muttered as if to herself, a note of contempt in her voice. It was such a different reaction that the men had a moment of hope. But then she shook her head and their hearts sank. "What kind of name? No, no Diavol."

The two men exchanged glances. Brandon took a wild chance before he quite realized what he was saying. "Listen, we're looking for him, but we're not his friends." His heart thudded in his chest. "We want to take him down."

Troy looked uncharacteristically rattled by Brandon's ad-lib, but he produced the handful of twenties that the baker and cafe waiter had declined. "Please, ma'am, anything you can tell us, anything at all …" He held the money out.

The woman looked at them with a combination of anger and disbelief. "Take down," she said in a sarcastic tone. "You take down who? Think you take down Dmytro Dovzhenko? Devil himself? So you can be new Diavol?" She practically spat as she said the name again. "Why should I help you?" She turned and shouted toward the door she'd emerged from. "Andriy!"

"No, we don't want to take over," explained Brandon desperately. "We—"

The back door swung open again and a man stepped through. He appeared to be in his forties or fifties and was shorter than both Troy and Brandon but powerfully built. He took one look at the woman and moved toward the two men, hands clenching into fists at his sides. Troy stood, looking at ease but alert.

"Andriy, you make them go," the old woman said, turning her back on them and their money.

"Wait, just hear me out," Troy said to the man. "We just want a little information about Diavol—what was the name, Dmitry?" he asked, looking over at the woman who now had her back resolutely turned toward them all. He proffered the money to Andriy this time. The man looked at it with scorn, and Brandon dug out his wallet and added several more twenties to the fistful of bills.

Andriy looked at it, then over at the old woman, and then glanced out the front door at the street. He jerked his head toward the kitchen door and strode to it, not bothering to check if the men followed. Brandon scrambled off his stool and he and Troy hurried after him.

# CHAPTER THIRTEEN

Large pots simmered, fragrant steam pouring off them, and piles of potatoes, onions, cabbages, and beets sat partly dismantled on long wooden surfaces. There was no one else in the room; it must have been the work of just Andriy and the woman.

Once the door had closed, the man turned on them and held out his hand. Troy pressed the wad of cash into it and it disappeared into the man's pocket. He folded his arms.

"After this, don't ever come back here again," Andriy said. "Agreed?"

Both men nodded eagerly.

"Diavol," the man said brusquely. "Real name's Dmytro Dovzhenko. Not many people know that. He does what he wants. His guys—you don't mess with them." Andriy glanced at the door they'd just come through. "Mama doesn't like to talk about him. My baby sister, she got caught up in his stuff. Went off with one of his men, got into drugs and who knows what. We haven't seen her in years."

"Do you know what his … 'stuff' is?" Troy pressed. "Just drugs, or other things?"

The man nodded. "Drugs, whores, guns, you name it," he said. "I try not to know too much. But you hear things. He doesn't show up much anymore, but he's got lots of guys to run things here."

"Out west?" Brandon asked.

The man shrugged. "I don't really—" he heard something through the door and his face sagged with sudden fear. He froze for a second, then gestured for them to follow him as he walked between the rows of burners and prep stations.

He reached a door at the back, opened it, and peered out, looking both ways. Then he stood back from the door and waved them through. "Don't let them see you or we're dead," he hissed. With that, the door swung shut quickly, but then closed gently as if he were holding it on the other side.

Brandon's heart was in his mouth, but Troy beckoned and he followed. They walked quickly through an alley littered with bits of food and crumpled paper and plastic. A ripe smell of rotting produce and meat clung to the hot air as they hurried the length of the block.

The street they turned onto was deserted. Brandon exhaled with relief, then started to laugh at his own paranoia.

Troy gestured for him to stay quiet, and the laughter died in his throat. Men's voices, conversing in low tones, drifted out of the alley they'd just left. Brandon couldn't make out any words but apparently Troy had picked something up. "Let's split up," he whispered. He gave Brandon the intersection where the rental car was located and told him to go ahead.

Brandon continued right, the way they'd come out, and started down a deserted backstreet with no storefronts, just dingy apartment buildings and small townhouses, some boarded up.

A shout rang out behind him and he flinched, looking back. He saw nothing but heard grunts and what could be the sound of fists making impact.

He stood rooted to the ground for a moment, torn between running and going back. He retraced his steps but stopped near a tree whose trunk was almost big enough to conceal him. Carefully he peered out from it, trying not to move too much.

A man lay on the sidewalk near the alley, moaning and holding his head with one hand. He staggered to his feet, swaying, just as two other men stumbled out of the alley, locked in a struggle. Brandon realized one was Troy—and his adversary had his neck in both hands.

Troy released his grip on the man's shoulder and instead forced his forearm between them, wedging it under the man's chin and pushing. As it slowly stifled his air supply, the man's hold on Troy's neck faltered, as did his balance. Troy took advantage of his firmer footing and rammed into the man, backing him against the wall behind him. Brandon heard the crack as the man's skull hit the wall; he seemed dazed but was still struggling.

Troy pulled him away from the wall and threw him to the ground on his back, then leapt on him and began throwing punches that made audible impact with his face.

The other man's swaying had subsided, and he jumped Troy from behind, kicking him in the ribs. Troy grunted and rolled off his one attacker, smoothly coming to his feet with an agility that startled Brandon. He slowly approached the man who'd kicked him, and the man backed away instinctively, then turned and bolted down the alley.

Troy returned his attention to the other man, but he lay still, seemingly knocked out. Troy scanned the street, braced for more attacks. His eyes stopped at the tree and Brandon realized he'd been seen. He stepped out, feeling nervous for some reason, and Troy's posture visibly relaxed. After one more glance at the unconscious man, he loped across the street and rejoined Brandon.

They got onto a busier street where Brandon felt safer surrounded by people. Walking briskly but not running, they soon reached their rental car at the edge of the neighborhood. As Troy fumbled for the keys, Brandon watched the street for anyone who seemed to be targeting them. He heard the door locks pop open and slid into the passenger side, relieved.

On the way out of D.C., Brandon felt himself shaking as the adrenaline slowly ebbed out of his body. Troy, who seemed to be suffering no such aftereffects despite his street brawl, glanced at him. "You OK?" he asked.

"That was fucked up," Brandon said. "You think they really were after us for asking about Diavol?"

"Not sure," Troy said, "Andriy thought so. I guess it's possible one of the other people we talked to made a call to someone." He shrugged with an astounding nonchalance.

"Hey," he said, "might as well see if you can find anything on that name. Dmytro Dovzhenko. It's a long shot, but you never know."

Brandon took out his phone and typed the name into a search engine, guessing at how to spell it. His search brought up a suggested alternate spelling.

He touched the surface of the phone to start scrolling through results, but paused at the top of the page. "Shit," he whispered to himself.

"What?" asked Troy, glancing over at him. He navigated into the parking lot of the motel and turned in to a spot near their room.

"No, that can't be the same guy." Brandon scrolled further down, then back up again. He clicked a top link and studied it.

"What is it?" Troy demanded. He turned off the ignition and reached for the phone. Brandon passed it to him.

"There's a football coach in the Ukraine by the same name," Brandon ventured. "But also … it has to be a coincidence." He leaned over and pointed at the page he'd just opened. "It's also the name of the Ukrainian ambassador to the United States."

# CHAPTER FOURTEEN

Back in their room, Troy made calls while Brandon ordered an early dinner. Except for the pastries and tea they'd had in Little Odessa, they'd had no lunch, and they were both suddenly starving.

While Troy talked, his voice low enough that the words were unintelligible, Brandon looked Dovzhenko up on his own phone again. If the ambassador was actually "Diavol," there was no sign other than what they'd heard in Little Odessa. Most links were news stories about corruption and political unrest in

Ukraine, with quotes from Dovzhenko about the work being done to stamp it out.

A four-year-old news story reported his appointment to his current post from deputy ambassador. He was fifty years old, Brandon learned from online biographies. He studied the photos of him—a stocky man verging on rotund, with receding dark hair and a mustache. Brandon scoured his bland, impassive face for any trace of menace.

Out of curiosity Brandon searched for "Diavol." The search engine yielded a translation first; it was Romanian for "devil." It meant the same thing in Ukrainian, spelled "dyyavol." A chill went down his spine.

The food was delivered, and Brandon left the room to buy sodas from the motel vending machine.

By the time he returned, Troy was off his phone. He shoveled shrimp fried rice and eggrolls into his mouth, filling in what he'd learned so far between bites. No one he'd spoken to had heard the nickname "Diavol" or any rumors of criminal activity associated with

Dovzhenko. Among diplomatic circles he had a reputation as an inveterate partier. His long-suffering wife spent most of her time in Ukraine, and their children were in boarding schools. He had plenty of freedom in the United States and took full advantage of it.

Troy's phone rang and he was off talking to another contact. Brandon finished eating and listened in to Troy's side of the conversation, which didn't reveal anything.

But when he hung up he looked serious and thoughtful. "We need to get back to Seattle as soon as possible. He's probably there now. We won't learn anything more here that we can't get there."

While Troy looked for tickets on a red-eye, Brandon took a hot shower to try and relax. He changed into his last clean pair of briefs and a pair of sweatshorts and lay down on his bed, tense but exhausted, while Troy showered too.

He came out of the bathroom in boxer briefs and damp hair, smelling of an aftershave that Brandon realized was already becoming familiar and—despite last night's betrayal—oddly comforting.

"Did I miss any calls?" Troy asked.

"Not that I heard," Brandon replied. He found himself stealing glances at Troy as he walked across the room and checked his phone. He kept replaying the day's events; he was shaken even from witnessing the fight, yet Troy seemed unaffected by it as he worked his connections and planned their next move. He seemed larger than life.

It made it all the more gut-wrenching that he'd stood by as Michael drugged him. Still, when Brandon thought of how he'd been stuck for weeks in the same hopeless cycle before encountering Troy, he was filled again with reluctant wonder and gratitude. His face flushed as the conflicting feelings coursed through him.

Troy looked over and caught him staring, and Brandon felt his face grow even hotter as their eyes locked for several seconds. He couldn't read Troy's face exactly, but a small smile seemed to play on his lips for a second.

Brandon looked away with a nervous flutter in his stomach that he couldn't explain.

Troy sat down on the other bed, facing him. Brandon put down his phone and sat up, eager to break what suddenly felt like a loaded silence. "So what else did you learn about this guy? That last call was pretty long."

Troy nodded. "Yeah, I lucked out, big time. This girl I used to date—her dad is State Department—got an aide to a diplomat from Poland to talk to me. He knew a lot about Dovzhenko and didn't hold back." He opened his soda and took a swig. "Apparently this aide, Stefan, had a—kind of a fling with Dovzhenko and was pretty bitter about how it ended."

"Huh!" said Brandon. "So he, uh—"

"Yep," Troy said. "Apparently Dovzhenko has a good thing going on here in America while his wife lives in Ukraine. And that thing just happens to be younger guys."

"Wow. Not … what I expected."

"Right? I didn't mention the whole 'Diavol' thing and he didn't bring up anything illegal with Dovzhenko, other than occasionally getting drugs for some of his boy toys."

"Doesn't seem like it can be the same guy at all," Brandon mused.

"I'd have thought that too, but the kicker is he said Dovzhenko spends a lot of time in Seattle, even has another apartment there. Stefan didn't know why exactly; he spent a few weekends with him there and said he guessed he just liked it. Easier to sleep around away from D.C. and less chance of his wife dropping in on him, or something. But that Seattle connection, that's just too coincidental."

"Right," Brandon said, taking it all in. "So what do we do now?"

"Well," Troy said, hesitating. "If he's who Nasreen relocated to investigate, it seems likely he does a lot more than party out there. You should know, she's not some run-of-the-mill agent—she only handles big cases. Complex, sensitive—like, you know, if an ambassador was involved in organized crime. I think we should try to locate him, find out where he goes, who he's in contact with in Seattle."

"That makes sense," Brandon said slowly, trying to come to grips with this new idea of Nasreen. "But how are we going to find him?"

"I couldn't get his Seattle address from Stefan; obviously I didn't want to ask for that. He thought I was just getting background on the guy for political shit. But he did happen to mention a club they spent a lot of time at when he was there: Purgatory. Heard of it?"

"It sounds familiar," Brandon said. "I've never been there, though." He typed the name in on his phone. "Three-level gay nightclub with dance floors and go-go dancers," he read aloud. "Sounds huge."

"Well, Stefan talked about a VIP area that Dovzhenko reserves when he goes there. So maybe it wouldn't be too hard to spot him."

"OK," Brandon agreed. "Then what?"

"Well ..." Troy hesitated again. "OK, this might sound crazy, but hear me out. Stefan gave me an earful about Dovzhenko's preferences. Apparently he tends to really go for tall blond guys. Stefan was very specific about this; said he doesn't fit the description and felt like that's why he got dropped. He bitched about how shallow Dovzhenko is. Like, for a long time."

Brandon laughed a little. "Explains your side of the conversation," he said. "You didn't get a chance to say much." He thought about what Troy had said, and something dawned on him. "Wait …" he said. "You're not thinking that I …?"

# CHAPTER FIFTEEN

Brandon's unfinished sentence hung in the air for an uncomfortable few seconds that felt longer. "I mean, I can't tell you what to do," Troy said at last. "But it's almost too perfect. If you could get near him, you might overhear something, find out more than we could just by tailing him."

Brandon considered it. Troy made a crazy kind of sense, but he couldn't imagine it. He didn't even know how to flirt with women properly, and he'd been working at that his entire adult life. "I wouldn't know where to start," he managed to say.

"I don't think you'd have to do much," Troy said. "I gotta be honest, you're pretty easy on the eyes. I doubt you've ever been to a gay bar before, because you'd probably know the kind of attention you'd get."

Brandon felt his face get hot again. His stomach was churning. The conversation was even more uncomfortable being seated inches away from a shirtless man who seemed to be having an effect on him he didn't expect. He blinked rapidly, trying to focus instead on what Troy was asking him to do. "OK … OK," he stammered, "but say that even worked and I got Dovzhenko's attention. I mean, what if he wanted me to, like, go home with him?"

Troy looked down at his phone. "I couldn't decide that for you," he said, sounding too matter-of-fact for what he was suggesting.

"Holy shit." Brandon couldn't believe they were even having this conversation.

"I know," Troy said. "It's not exactly— pleasant to think about, especially if this guy is mixed up in—whatever's happened to Nasreen. If you want me to try instead, I can. I just thought with you fitting his type, you'd have a way better chance than me."

"It's not just that this guy's probably some kind of supervillain—I mean, that's bad enough—but I just wouldn't even know, I've never—I'm straight, dude!"

Troy turned his eyes back to him, a long, considering look. "Are you?" he asked, sounding a little amused. "I was kind of starting to think you were, I don't know, *into* me." He shrugged and turned his attention back to his phone.

Brandon was at a loss for words. He knew he'd been exclusively interested in women his whole life; he supposed he'd occasionally admired men's bodies casually, but he'd never seriously been attracted to one. So how exactly could he describe what Troy made him feel? He didn't know and couldn't deal with it, or the other, equally bizarre idea Troy had thrown out, the crazy plan to get close to Dovzhenko.

"It's like I said." Brandon's head was spinning as he tried to address both thoughts. "I'm not—I've never done anything with …

This guy, from what it sounds like, he'd know I wasn't gay. He could tell I didn't know what I was doing. I *wouldn't* know what I was doing." He shook his head. "It would never work."

Troy smiled a little at his phone. "Gay guys don't have ESP," he said gently, "and they don't expect every guy to be super experienced or do the exact same things."

*What are we even talking about?* Brandon thought incredulously. "How would you know?" he blurted. "Have *you* ever—?" he stopped, too embarrassed to finish.

There was another brief silence between the two of them. Troy turned his eyes to Brandon, the smile still on his lips. "Yeah."

"Oh," Brandon said. Now he felt embarrassed for a different reason. "That's, uh, that's totally cool. Sorry, I didn't mean to—I guess I just assumed that you and Nasreen were—like—"

"Uh-huh," Troy said as Brandon struggled to find words to complete the sentence. "That too." He pressed his lips together as if to suppress a laugh. "You know some people go both ways, right?"

Brandon lay back on his bed, staring at the ceiling.

"You OK?" he heard Troy say.

"Yeah," he said, trying to sound normal though he felt anything but. "It's a lot to think about, I guess."

"Talk to me," Troy said. "We might as well be straight with each other, right?"

*Like you were when I got drugged?* Brandon thought with some bitterness. But he set that aside and sorted through his other feelings, trying to put words to them. "I guess you probably know I'm—kind of in love with Nasreen. Right?" After his drug-induced oversharing, how could Troy not know? He glanced over to see Troy's typically implacable expression had returned. At least he wasn't openly laughing at him now.

Troy nodded. "Yeah, I can tell."

Brandon nodded in return, going back to staring at the ceiling. "You know, so it's just—a little hard. Since you were with her first. And I don't know where I stand with her. Or—" his voice grew husky with suppressed tears "—whether any of that even matters now if she's …" he trailed off, remembering Troy's admonition not to think about that possibility.

"Hey," Troy said in a sympathetic tone. "I get it, it's a weird situation. If it makes you feel any better, about that part anyway, I've never had any problem with Nasreen seeing someone else when we're apart. I still don't. And she knew that I'd be OK with it. So she didn't do anything wrong, as far as I'm concerned."

"Thanks for that," Brandon said. And he did feel some relief. Even though he felt jealous, and hurt that Nasreen hadn't told him any of this, it did make the situation feel a little less wrong. "I was worried you were pissed off about that." He wanted to ask more about Troy's relationship with Nasreen, to figure out what it meant for him, but talking about her when he wasn't even sure she was alive just seemed fraught with pain, so he left it at that.

"Good," Troy said. "And as for that other thing—trying to meet Dovzhenko—you don't have to decide right away, and I won't blame you if you say no. We have other options."

"OK," Brandon said, feeling another wave of relief. "Thanks—sorry. It's a lot to take in. I appreciate having more time."

He felt Troy's eyes on him and looked over almost unwillingly. He knew there was one more thing they hadn't talked about, and he had no idea what to do about it. Troy's expression was typically unreadable, and Brandon felt helpless to look away.

Troy finally broke the spell by standing. "Hey, I just remembered something," he said. He went to a dresser drawer and got out a bottle of whiskey. "I got this yesterday and totally forgot about it." He grabbed two plastic cups from the sink outside their shared bathroom, tore the plastic wrappers off them and poured. "Here," he said, bringing one to Brandon. He stood by the bed, sipped his drink, and watched as Brandon sat up, accepted the other cup, and drank his whole shot in a gulp. "Feel better?" he asked.

"Yeah, kind of," Brandon said, enjoying the warm feeling spreading through him. "Thanks."

"Anything else you need to get off your chest?" Troy asked with a little smile.

Brandon lowered his eyes self-consciously. "Not that I can think of," he mumbled.

Just then he heard the springs creak and felt the mattress sink a little on his right-hand side as Troy sat next to him on his bed. He was afraid to turn his head; his eyes were stuck staring at the floor. The hair on the nape of his neck prickled as he imagined Troy looking at him, though he wasn't sure if he was or, if so, how he felt about it. He stood abruptly and went to the bottle of whiskey, poured himself a heftier shot. He turned and held the bottle up. "More?" he said.

"Sure," Troy said, holding his cup up. Brandon brought the bottle over and started to pour, suddenly hyperaware that he was standing very close to Troy with only shorts on and that Troy was seated on his bed wearing even less.

Troy smiled up at him, and Brandon was mesmerized by the little lines that formed at the sides of his mouth and crinkled the corners of his eyes. He almost overfilled the tiny cup, stopped himself, and carefully set the bottle on the bedside table.

As he was doing so, he felt Troy's free hand touch his belly lightly, then slide up toward his chest.

# CHAPTER SIXTEEN

Brandon started a little at the sudden contact, then found he couldn't move. And felt a little shocked to realize he didn't want to. The light touch seemed to spread warmth through his body even faster than the shot of whiskey had. His heart felt like it was pounding at about four times its normal speed, and his breathing was fast and shallow.

He somehow managed to meet Troy's gaze again as the man looked up at him. His eyes were full of warmth and a bit of humor. "Finish your drink so you don't spill it," Troy said, still moving his free hand slowly over

Brandon's skin, trailing down toward his left hip, as he downed his own shot and let the plastic cup fall to the floor.

Brandon hesitated, then tossed back his second shot and threw his cup away too. His whole body was tingling from Troy's touch and he didn't want it to end, but he stood helplessly, realizing he had no idea what to do or even how to respond.

As if sensing his confusion, Troy gripped his arms and pulled gently but firmly. Brandon hesitantly knelt until he was the one looking up into Troy's eyes, and the man leaned forward and kissed him on the mouth.

Brandon felt shockwaves through his system. The feel of Troy's warm, firm lips and the slight abrasiveness of invisible stubble against his face was like nothing he'd ever experienced. He touched Troy's strong thighs, tentatively at first, feeling his hard muscles under his skin.

Troy pulled him closer until he was pressed against him. "This OK with you?" he asked.

Brandon nodded, feeling dizzy. "Yeah," he said in a whisper. "But I don't know what to do."

Troy kissed him again. "I'll show you," he whispered back. He took Brandon's right hand from his thigh and pressed it against the swelling in his briefs. Brandon's breath caught in his throat as he allowed Troy to manipulate his hand, helping him grip and rub the bulge through the thin cloth. Troy edged his briefs off and moved Brandon's hands back to the newly freed erection. He marveled at the impossibly soft skin and the hardness it encased. He felt Troy's hand cup the back of his head, gently encouraging him to move closer. He hesitated, but his curiosity to know what it felt like was irresistible. He lowered his head.

Brandon felt lost in an alternate reality. Part of him seemed to be hovering above what was happening, observing as if from a distance. Troy let go of his head and leaned back, his hands gripping the bedspread.

When Brandon took a break, Troy helped him to his feet and then pushed him onto the bed on his back, pulling off his shorts and briefs. Brandon closed his eyes. Every nerve in his body felt attuned to what Troy was doing with his mouth and hands.

He felt a warmth gathering and focusing inside him, and his muscles tightened in anticipation. But Troy pulled back before it could build to a climax, leaving him feeling frantic.

"Not yet," he said with a knowing grin. "Stay where you are." He got up and went to the dresser. Brandon watched, breathing heavily but not moving, as Troy extracted a condom from his wallet. He tensed but didn't object when Troy returned to the bed. He felt something impossibly large press against him and wondered how it would ever happen. Troy leaned over him and whispered, "Relax." Then he knelt up again and began to massage Brandon's erection, and the tender nerve endings sent sensations through his entire body. Overwhelmed, he felt himself slowly opening to Troy's gentle insistence while quickly approaching his own climax at the same time.

When Brandon came, Troy was finally able to push fully into him. Brandon saw black bursts like fireworks against the lids of his closed eyes; as his orgasm ebbed away, new sensations were taking over; new parts of his body coming to life. Discomfort gave way to a new kind of pleasure. Troy had started out careful and gentle but his movements took on an uncontrollable urgency, and Brandon opened his eyes in time to see Troy squeeze his shut. He groaned and dropped onto the bed next to Brandon.

The two men lay panting audibly side by side, Brandon's arm flung over his eyes.

"You OK?" he heard Troy say again.

"Uh-huh," Brandon said hoarsely.

"We should get some rest now," said Troy. He got up and went to the bathroom, and Brandon heard water running. He turned off the light between the beds and lay in the semi-darkness, staring at the ceiling.

Troy returned from the bathroom and went to his own bed. He picked his phone up. "I'll set an alarm for two-thirty," he said, sounding as matter-of-fact as if nothing had happened. "We need to drop the car off and then get a cab to the airport. Try to get some sleep, OK?"

"Mm-hmm," Brandon said. Apparently inarticulate noises were all he could manage. He curled up and pulled the covers over himself; the air-conditioned room suddenly felt colder than he could bear.

* * *

He wasn't sure how much he'd slept, if at all. When the alarm went off, at first Brandon could barely drag his eyes open. Then he felt a certain painful tenderness and the night's events came back to him. A jolt of adrenaline brought him fully awake in a heartbeat. He looked over at Troy, who was sitting up and scrubbing his face. Brandon realized they were both still undressed. He avoided looking over any more as he hunted for his briefs, finding them on the floor by the bed.

As he pulled on his clothes and packed the remainder of his belongings in his backpack, always averting his eyes from wherever Troy was at the moment, his mind went over and over the night before. A mixture of shame and residual excitement coursed through his veins.

Troy also got ready in silence. They looked around the room one more time. The only thing left was the bottle of whiskey, still more than half full. It stood on the night table like an emblem of what had happened between them.

"OK," Brandon said, still avoiding looking at Troy, "we good?"

Troy shrugged off his backpack, which had been slung on one shoulder, and dropped it to the floor. "Almost," he said. He grabbed Brandon by the shoulders and pulled him into a hug. It was friendly but longer and somehow more intimate than any embrace Brandon had ever had with another man. He returned the gesture hesitantly. Troy pulled back, cupped Brandon's face in his hands, and planted a long, tender kiss on his lips. Brandon, surprised, nonetheless found himself closing his eyes and leaning into it.

Troy stepped back and smiled. "Last night was great," he said. Brandon couldn't help but return the smile, though he didn't know if it was better or worse than pretending it hadn't happened.

They returned the rental car and ordered a ride from there. The pitch black night began softening to gray as their driver approached the airport.

* * *

The cabin was quiet as most of the passengers napped, including Brandon's seatmate, a middle-aged man in a rumpled suit whose nose whistled softly in his sleep.

Troy was somewhere ahead of Brandon out of sight; once again their last-minute ticket purchases hadn't given them the option to sit together. Brandon felt a bit relieved; being near Troy on the cab ride to the airport had brought a rush of confused feelings. Though it hadn't occurred to him at the time, part of him wondered whether what had happened was some kind of sick test or preparation for the plan they'd discussed. Which made it feel especially wrong that he'd ended up enjoying it. Even away from Troy he kept flashing back to the night before; sitting next to him and smelling his aftershave would have made it worse.

As they drew closer to home, he forced himself to consider Troy's idea. As wildly out of character as it would be for him, it made just enough sense that he couldn't dismiss it outright. Dovzhenko would hopefully have his guard down if he was out partying. He probably wouldn't suspect someone he was flirting with to have any connection to whatever was going on with Nasreen.

And anyway, Brandon couldn't think of anything he'd done in the past few weeks that had been *in* character for him. His life seemed unrecognizable when compared with anything he'd ever done before.

Even his time with Nasreen had been a leap forward for him; never before had he been with anyone who challenged him to think more deeply about issues, to question his assumptions and sheltered worldview. At the same time, he'd learned more from her about giving and receiving pleasure than he'd picked up over a lifetime of dating.

Thinking about that took him down a train of thought. Would last night have even been possible had Nasreen not done away with so much of his inexperience and inhibitions?

He wondered for a moment if he'd have been better off not having met her and staying in his comfortable rut. But it didn't matter because here he was. And he still felt grateful for all she'd shown him and taught him and made him open to. Including Troy, he thought. Maybe.

And if she'd made him capable of so much, maybe he could do this. Maybe he owed it to her to try.

* * *

That night, he found himself standing in line to get into Purgatory.

# CHAPTER SEVENTEEN

When Brandon had first told him of his decision, as they walked through the airport after disembarking, Troy had looked a little surprised, he thought, but immediately started planning their next move.

They'd discussed going in together, but Troy decided it would be better for Brandon to be alone—easier to approach, he said—and besides, he thought it wise that Dovzhenko didn't see him. That way he could tail him or approach him in another situation, if need be, and not be recognized.

The rest of their plan was simple. Brandon would try to catch Dovzhenko's attention and, if successful, stay close to him as long as possible, watching and listening for clues as to whether he really was Diavol.

Troy would watch the entrance of the club and follow if he saw Brandon leave with anyone. If Brandon was in trouble, he'd text and add "911" to his message.

They'd attempted to get more rest at Brandon's before night fell. Brandon had found himself wondering if Troy would try to join him in his bedroom. He felt relieved but almost a little let down when the man headed to the guest room without a hint of considering any other option.

Brandon managed to doze fitfully for part of the afternoon. When he got up, Troy was already in the living room.

"Did you get any sleep?" he asked. Brandon wobbled his hand in a so-so gesture and went to the kitchen to make coffee. Troy followed. "How are you feeling?" he said. His tone was casual but Brandon thought he detected a note of concern.

Brandon shrugged. "Fine, I guess," he said, his own voice belying that statement.

"Nervous?" Troy asked.

"Trying not to be," Brandon said. He got the coffeemaker going and turned to Troy in time to see a look of concern before the man rearranged his features closer to his usual inscrutable expression. "Hey, it's fine," Brandon said. "I doubt anything's gonna happen anyway."

Troy laughed a little. "Yeah," he said. "This whole plan is full of long shots, so it might be a real let-down."

"I'd be kind of relieved," Brandon said. He regretted his words as soon as they came out of his mouth. Troy seemed so fearless, and Brandon wanted to at least not seem like too much of a coward and feel like he was doing his share to find Nasreen. "I didn't mean that. I'd rather something happens so we can find something out."

He went into the living room and Troy trailed after him. "Well, um, just remember you can call me in anytime you need to, OK?"

Brandon nodded, trying to smile naturally. "I know," he said. "It's no big deal, really. Whatever happens, I'll be fine."

The hours dragged and flew by simultaneously. Then it was time. Troy drove Brandon's car to the club and dropped him off, then left to park out of sight as he got in line.

Brandon tried not to fidget or look self-conscious as he waited. Ahead of and behind him, groups of men (and the occasional woman) talked and laughed excitedly. He stared at the ground, feeling like he was in a strange dream, and shuffled slowly forward whenever the line moved.

At last Brandon arrived at the front of the line, and a bouncer checked ID and stamped his hand. "Pay in there," he said, gesturing behind him.

As Brandon paid his entrance fee, he asked the man behind the counter if there was a VIP area. The man looked him over dismissively.

"Third floor," he said. "It's already been reserved though."

Brandon thanked him and entered the club.

Past a deserted coat check and through an open doorway he reached the main dance floor of the club. Auto-tuned vocals rang out over a hypnotic beat. Despite the line he'd been in, the floor was half empty. The club seemed to only just be coming to life.

He wound his way easily through the crowd, noticing that quite a few men tried to catch his eye as he passed. He supposed that was a good sign. He'd worried over his basic wardrobe, but Troy had assured him a T-shirt and jeans would be fine.

He found a staircase on the other side and took it to the second floor. There a smaller dance floor butted up against a stage where three young guys in brightly colored G-strings and practically identical buff bodies writhed. Hands reached up from the crowd in front of them, tucking bills into the waistbands of their underwear and sometimes copping a feel while they were there.

Brandon stood and watched from a corner for a few minutes, wondering how they felt about being groped by multiple strangers. He couldn't tell from their expressions or their movements.

Another stairway led up to the third floor, and he took it. The music was slower up here, more atmospheric. The lighting was mellower too. A long bar spanned one side of the large space, and the floor was scattered with high-top tables, most without chairs. A few large pillars, which might have been purely ornamental, were encircled by curved padded benches. Men stood or sat together in self-aware poses, as if they were constantly being photographed.

On one side of the room, Brandon saw a raised section with two stairs leading up to it, bracketed off by velvet ropes and furnished with plush leather sofas and chairs.

He ordered a drink at the bar and wandered to the table closest to the VIP area. Trying not to stare, he took short glances while pretending to scan the whole room.

A small group occupied the area, less than fifteen, he estimated. The next time he looked, he saw it was a mixed group; several men in the corner were chatting up women. A few other men sat in a group near the center of the area, a bucket with a bottle poking out of it on the table.

Brandon ignored the VIP section for a little while, then glanced back again. He studied a few of the faces. Many of them seemed about his age or younger, but there were a couple of older men. One in particular … he turned away, acting like he was surveying other parts of the bar. Finally he looked over again.

This time he focused on the man who had caught his attention. He was in profile, sitting on one side of a large loveseat. A younger man was perched on the armrest next to him, looking quite drunk and waving a cocktail glass in the air as he said something Brandon couldn't make out. He looked more closely at the older man—balding in front, dark hair and mustache, stocky build … Brandon got his phone out and looked up Dmytro Dovzhenko again. He studied the photos, looked casually around, then back at the VIP area again.

His stomach seized up with both excitement and anxiety. He put his phone away. Then he pulled it out again and texted Troy: "I see him."

He held his phone until it vibrated twice, signaling a new message. "Contact?"

It felt good to be messaging with someone friendly when he felt like he was in enemy territory. "No. Not sure what 2do"

His phone buzzed and he looked at it. "Just b urself"

It vibrated again shortly. "aka look super hot"

Brandon laughed a little. "U sure that'll work?" he wrote back.

The response came quick. "100%"

Then: "Worked on me right?"

He read the messages over and over again, his pulse racing, his face feeling a little warm. He somehow couldn't believe Troy had written that; it's not as if they'd flirted at all or made any mention of their night at the motel since they got back to Seattle. He didn't know what to write but sent a smiley emoticon so Troy wouldn't think he was put off by the exchange. Then he forced himself to slip the phone in his pocket.

He looked up, still smiling a little—and caught Dovzhenko watching him.

# CHAPTER EIGHTEEN

Brandon tried not to overreact. He let himself be held by the man's gaze for several moments. He broadened his smile slightly, then turned away casually and went to the bar to get another drink. He seemed to feel the man's eyes on his back, though he wasn't sure he was really being watched.

He strolled slowly back to the same table with his second drink. Soon he caught Dovzhenko watching him again. He met the man's eyes again, looked away, then looked back. Dovzhenko was leaned over, talking to one of the other men. Brandon glanced down, wondering how much he could look over there without starting to look suspicious. He gazed aimlessly around the room, sipping his drink.

"Good evening," a heavily accented voice said in his ear. He jumped and turned; the man Dovzhenko had been talking to was standing right beside him. He had similar dark hair and a mustache, so for a split second Brandon had thought it *was* Dovzhenko.

"You snuck up on me!" Brandon said, trying to sound lighthearted. "Hi there." His heart was in his mouth.

"How are you doing tonight?" the man asked pleasantly.

"Pretty good," Brandon said, searching for something to say. "Kind of bored. My friends I was meeting here aren't coming after all."

"Oh, that's too bad," the man said. "I'm Vitaliy." He held out his hand, and Brandon shook it. "Since you are left all alone tonight, would you like to join my friends instead?" He gestured toward the VIP area.

Brandon could hardly believe his ears. "Oh, um …" he said, trying to decide how soon to agree, and also feeling like he'd rather run away.

"I can assure you we don't bite," the man said in a laughing tone. Brandon laughed too, hoping it sounded real.

"Well, uh, what the hell," he said brightly. "Sure, Vitaliy. My name is Brandon, by the way." He and Troy had discussed using a fake name and concluded it was too complicated and posed a danger of him forgetting. As long as he just used his first name, they figured it wasn't too much identifying information.

The man smiled. "Brandon, it's nice to meet you. Come with me, please." He led him over to the VIP section and pulled back the rope, waving him in with a flourish.

Brandon entered and smiled at the men who turned to look at him. Vitaliy introduced him and Brandon waved. He caught a few names above the music and soon forgot them. The younger men seemed to mainly be interested in drinking and flirting. He hoped he wasn't wrong about that; he hoped he wouldn't regret not trying harder to remember their names.

Vitaliy took Brandon's arm and turned him to face the one man he was trying not to stare at too obviously. "Brandon, I'd like you to meet my friend Dmytro. Dmytro, this is Brandon."

Dovzhenko turned and looked him up and down. Brandon tried to keep looking lighthearted and matter-of-fact as he said, "Nice to meet you—Dmytro, was it?"

At last Dovzhenko smiled and held out his hand. "You can call me Demi. Nice to meet you, too." His accent was less pronounced than Vitaliy's, like he'd been in America a lot longer.

"Excuse me for a minute," Dovzhenko said to him, and beckoned Vitaliy to lean close. He whispered something in his ear and Vitaliy nodded.

Seconds later, he was smoothly escorting the drunk young man from the armrest of Dovzhenko's side of the loveseat. The young man barely seemed to know what was happening as he wobbled down the stairs and was deposited onto one of the circular benches near some other men.

Dovzhenko showed no interest in watching him go; Brandon had his full attention now. "Forgive my young friend," he said. "He had a little too much to drink, I believe."

"No problem," Brandon said.

"Please, sit," Dovzhenko said. He gestured to the spot next to him on the loveseat, and Brandon sat down. "What are you drinking?"

"Vodka tonic," Brandon said, looking at his nearly empty glass.

"Ah, then you must try this vodka," Dovzhenko said, taking the glass from him and setting it down. He pulled the bottle out of the bucket on the table and picked up a clean cocktail glass. "You won't need any tonic, I promise you. It is very nice on its own." He poured a healthy amount into the glass and passed it to Brandon, who made a show of sipping it appreciatively.

"Very nice," Brandon said. "Thank you, it's delicious." He felt afraid that his fake friendliness would raise alarm bells, but the older man smiled as if flattered.

He leaned toward Dovzhenko in what he hoped looked like genuine interest in him. "So what do you do for a living, Demi?"

"I am a businessman," he responded. "I have many international dealings, import and export, you know, that sort of thing." He laid a hand on Brandon's knee. "It is a very prosperous time to be in business."

Brandon feigned an increased interest, assuming that was meant to impress him. Inside, he was chilled at the thought of what Dovzhenko might be importing and exporting. He did think it was interesting that the man didn't bring up his ambassadorship, which would have been a prestigious talking point; maybe he wanted to keep that a secret, or separate from this part of his life. Brandon suddenly wondered if that was another reason his fling with the Polish diplomat's aide hadn't lasted long.

They exchanged more small talk; Brandon mainly agreed with and acted interested in whatever Dovzhenko said, hoping the older man would keep the conversation going.

He tried to pay attention to the others seated in the VIP area as well. He got the sense that the men with women accompanying them were bodyguards of some sort; they kept an eye on everything going on, staying separate from the cluster of men at the center of the area.

As he spoke, Dovzhenko trailed his fingers along Brandon's bicep and forearm. Brandon knew he should seem interested in that too, so Dovzhenko didn't get bored and move on to someone else. He was reluctant to encourage him, but he didn't see any other way; it was either that or walk away from the situation.

He thought of Nasreen and steeled himself. Inching closer to Dovzhenko, he gradually changed position until his leg was pressed against the other man's. The next time Dovzhenko reached toward him, Brandon responded, touching the man's forearm in what he hoped was a casually flirtatious way.

Dovzhenko leaned over to whisper in his ear, "Do you need more to drink?" Brandon felt the man's mustache brush against him and his teeth nip his earlobe, then his neck. He closed his eyes, pretending to respond favorably.

"No thanks; I don't want to end up like your friend," he said lightly, gesturing toward the young man who had been ushered out of the VIP section and was now leaning, semiconscious, on the shoulder of another man.

Dovzhenko chuckled. "Good thinking," he purred. "In that case, if you have had enough, perhaps you would like to go somewhere else with me."

Brandon's stomach clenched with nerves. "Maybe," he said, trying to sound playful. "Where were you thinking we should go?"

The man's eyes swept greedily over Brandon's body. "My place."

Brandon smiled, hoping his tension didn't show. "You work fast," he said.

"When I see something I want, yes," Dovzhenko replied. "And when I get what I want, I return the favor." He ran his hand down Brandon's chest and stomach. "You give me something nice tonight, I get you something nice tomorrow. Hmm?" Brandon's insides lurched again. The thing that had felt like a remote possibility now seemed all but a sure thing, if he consented.

He thought about excusing himself to go to the bathroom and then slipping out quietly. It was a delightful prospect.

"What do you say?" Dovzhenko said, a note of impatience under his pleasant tone.

Brandon's heart sank as he heard himself say, "I'd like that."

# CHAPTER NINETEEN

"Excellent." Dovzhenko smiled triumphantly. "Vitaliy!" he called. "We leave now."

The entire group in the VIP area mobilized with precision. Some of the young men were sent away and dispersed into the larger lounge area. Vitaliy kept one by his side. The henchmen, as Brandon had come to think of the men on the outskirts of the group, gathered their ladies and led the way out.

They took a discreet elevator to the ground floor and exited through the main doors. One of the henchmen spoke to someone at the curb, who signaled two young men, handed them sets of car keys and sent them off at a jog.

While they waited for the cars, Brandon stood on the corner looking at the street. He couldn't see Troy but hoped he was out there watching and had spotted him. He wished too late that he'd gone to the restroom so he could alert Troy.

Two black SUVs pulled up one after the other. Brandon followed Dovzhenko into the back seat of one, and two of the henchmen got in the front. The rest of the party piled into the second vehicle.

In the quiet of the car, Brandon shifted uncomfortably. He wasn't sure how to strike a balance between seeming interested while not escalating the flirtation any more than necessary.

Dovzhenko ignored him at first anyway, talking to the men in the front seats in Ukrainian. His cloyingly friendly tone with Brandon was replaced by a cold, inflectionless voice that chilled him. The men responded with few words, and he saw the driver's eyes on him in the rearview mirror. He was momentarily gripped by icy dread, absolutely certain that they'd known what his game was all along and were now taking him to his death. Was this the SUV that had taken Nasreen away, which he'd now foolishly entered of his own free will?

Dovzhenko relaxed back against the seat, and the front seat passenger turned on a music station playing standard pop fare. "Business never stops, you know?" he said to Brandon, back to speaking English in his flirtatious voice. He grabbed Brandon's hand and put it on his own ample thigh. "But now we can play."

Brandon exhaled in quiet relief. He forced a smile and massaged the man's leg while Dovzhenko leaned in to kiss his neck again. He was unnerved at how quickly this was happening. And that it was so different from how he'd felt with Troy the night before.

But in a way that encounter made it easier. The experience gave him a reference point while he went through the motions. And since he felt nothing like he had with Troy, he was able to look at it as a purely practical measure to get the man to hopefully let his guard down and reveal something.

That calmed him, and he returned Dovzhenko's caresses more confidently. He still felt awkward, especially when he caught the driver watching him in the rearview with mild distaste, but what he was doing seemed to be working on Dovzhenko, so he focused on that.

He wasn't sure how long the drive actually took; it felt simultaneously interminable and like it was over too quickly. They arrived at a tall, modern building and drove into a parking garage underneath it.

The group got out of the two vehicles and headed toward an elevator bank. Brandon wondered how long there would be a crowd of people with them. He appreciated the reprieve, however long it lasted.

On the thirtieth floor, they left the elevator. There looked to be only two units on the floor, and one of the henchmen used a keycard to open one.

The door opened on a spacious living area with floor-to-ceiling windows and stunning views. Lights twinkled from other skyscrapers in the darkness.

Frosted bottles of vodka as well as beers and wines appeared, and a tray of cheeses, crackers and caviar. It all seemed to happen magically around them as Dovzhenko coasted through the bustling preparations, holding Brandon's elbow to guide him to a sofa. Brandon sank into its comfortable depths with Dovzhenko settling close beside him. The man leaned in toward him. "You have a most beautiful mouth," he whispered to Brandon. "I would like to see what it can do."

Brandon couldn't conceal his startled look as he glanced around at the other people beginning to trickle into the living room area where he and Dovzhenko sat. The man laughed at his expression and said, "Later, of course. When we're alone."

"Oh," Brandon said, relieved and full of dread at the same time. "Right." He regained his composure. "Later," he said, and leaned over to kiss Dovzhenko's neck.

The man chuckled again. A plate of snacks and two tumblers of ice cold vodka were brought to them and placed on the table in front of them. Dovzhenko spooned some caviar onto a cracker and held it up to Brandon, who took it obligingly into his mouth. As he chewed, experiencing the unfamiliar flavors and textures, he saw the man looking hungrily at his lips. He nervously sipped vodka.

The party continued for another hour or so, but Brandon was monopolized by Dovzhenko and didn't get up except once to get to the bathroom. While in there, he took advantage of the privacy and texted Troy, "I'm OK. with D." He checked the maps app on his phone and added the address that it showed him at.

He got a response: "i saw. im close. wut floor." Brandon texted "30" back.

He was washing his hands when his phone buzzed lightly. "U rly ok?"

He dried his hands. Reluctantly he typed "yeah all good"

Another alert. He read it. "U 911, I'll be there 2 mins. All night anytime"

His heart was full. He'd give anything to have Troy rescue him now. He shook his head to try and banish the thought. It was time to go back in. He texted simply "OK thx," then pocketed his phone and went back to Dovzhenko.

The others swirled around them for a short while longer, but Dovzhenko was getting more forward, reaching under Brandon's shirt and moving his hand farther up his thigh. He soon gave a signal to Vitaliy, who started clearing everyone out. "Next door, let's go everyone."

Before they left, one of the henchmen approached the couch. "Boss, I should check him."

Dovzhenko sighed. "Yes, all right." He looked almost apologetically at Brandon. "They are very protective."

While Brandon was puzzling over what he could mean, the man grabbed him by the shoulders and lifted him unceremoniously to his feet. Before Brandon knew what was happening, he felt the man's hands sliding along his back and sides, up the insides of his legs, patting and squeezing his crotch.

Brandon fought the urge to resist and stood there, looking questioningly at Dovzhenko, who gave him a little shrug and smile.

The henchman released him. "OK, he's clean," the man said. "Call if you need us, boss."

With that he left, and Brandon and Dovzhenko were fully alone for the first time. Brandon still stood, feeling off balance from what had happened.

Dovzhenko looked at him sympathetically. "It's nothing personal," he said. "They get nervous about leaving me with a stranger, so they make sure. In business, you understand, you can't be too careful."

Brandon laughed incredulously. "Well, that was a new experience," he said.

Dovzhenko reached out his hands, still relaxed on the couch. "Baby, come here," he said in a comforting voice. "It's OK, it's nothing. If I had my way he wouldn't have done that, but I appreciate their caution so I let them."

Brandon sat back down and Dovzhenko hugged him in a show of concern. Then he pulled away and cupped Brandon's face in his hands. "Now," he breathed. "We are alone at last. Can I see if your mouth is as talented as it is beautiful?"

# CHAPTER TWENTY

There was little time to mentally prepare, but being intoxicated made it seem less real. Dovzhenko leaned back expectantly. Brandon started unfastening the man's trousers with slightly trembling hands, trying to smile. Underneath he found silk boxers and fumbled in the fly.

He tried to reconjure the dispassionate attitude he'd had in the car on the way over. Judging from the man's response, it would be over soon. But then Dovzhenko's phone rang in his pocket, quite near Brandon's head. Dovzhenko took it out, looked at it, and sighed, then reluctantly pushed Brandon away and stood. "I apologize. I must take this," he said.

Brandon heard Dovzhenko talking in Ukrainian again as he approached the kitchen area. Brandon took out his own phone, opened an audio recording app and turned it on. He pretended to surf aimlessly as he let it record. He hoped it would pick up some of Dovzhenko's half of the conversation.

He heard Dovzhenko approach, using a tone that sounded like the call was winding down. Brandon stopped the recording app and flipped to something else.

He looked up as the other man returned and put his phone away. Dovzhenko smiled possessively down at him. "What was I thinking, going so fast? Come, let's go to my bedroom."

Brandon stood obediently and followed him down a short hallway to another room. It too had full-length windows and cold tile floors, as well as a giant bed with white and gold headboard and matching covers.

Dovzhenko lay back on the bed and Brandon approached tentatively, but the man held his hand up. "Take your clothes off first," he said commandingly.

Brandon stood where he was. He willed himself not to hesitate, and pulled his shirt off.

"More slowly," Dovzhenko directed. Brandon pasted a smile on his face and unfastened his jeans at a slower pace, edging them off and pulling his socks and shoes off at the same time. He stood for a second in his briefs, then slid them down his legs and stepped out of them. The large curtainless windows made him feel exposed and self-conscious, but he tried to look at ease.

Dovzhenko's self-satisfied smile faltered a little. "You are not aroused?" he said with a hint of petulance.

Brandon cast about for something to say. "I, uh, I was, but the phone call kind of ruined the mood a little bit, I guess."

"Well," Dovzhenko said, somewhat appeased, "you should remedy that now."

After a moment to process what that meant, Brandon took a breath and reached down. He closed his eyes so he couldn't see Dovzhenko watching and pictured Nasreen; her ripe hips pressed against him, her firm breasts cupped in his hands. Then his mind conjured an unexpected image of her pinned to a bed by Troy.

"Much better," he heard Dovzhenko say, and opened his eyes. The man was now completely undressed. "Now come here."

Brandon came toward the bed and climbed on, holding onto wisps of the scene he'd just imagined. He lay down, mentally steeling himself, and felt Dovzhenko approach him from behind.

"Wait!" he said, twisting around and looking back. He saw that Dovzhenko wasn't wearing protection. The thought of unprotected sex with this man sent cold fear through him. "Could you put a rubber on?"

Dovzhenko looked mildly annoyed, then purred, "I prefer it much better without."

"Please," Brandon said.

He watched with trepidation as the man's expression darkened further. Then, without warning, his face cleared and his smile returned.

"Well, if it will make you feel better," Dovzhenko said expansively. "If you have one; I don't."

Brandon scrambled off the bed and fumbled in the pocket of his jeans. He'd felt ridiculous putting condoms in his wallet, but now he was glad.

He came back to the bed and slid it onto Dovzhenko himself so he wouldn't have any reason to hesitate about wearing it. Then he resumed his position on his stomach on the bed, feeling as if he was willingly participating in a crime against himself.

He closed his eyes as Dovzhenko began. He thought about Troy the night before and the way he'd kissed him that morning. The images relaxed him somewhat and he was able to yield to Dovzhenko. It was painful but not unbearable. He focused on the knowledge that it would end.

Dovzhenko leaned heavily on him. "You like that?" he panted.

"Yes," Brandon whispered.

"You like—me—fucking—you—" Dovzhenko grunted, more of a statement than a question. On the final word, he groaned and pressed into Brandon hard for a second, then flopped onto the bed.

Brandon lay still, shell-shocked. Then he felt Dovzhenko's hand cupping his ass, gripping and squeezing. "You are very quiet when you make love," the man's voice said, back to its normal ingratiating tone.

"Am I?" Brandon managed to say. "I'm sorry."

"No, it's quite all right," Dovzhenko said. "You are a quiet boy, I can tell, but I like it." He chuckled. "You don't say much, you don't get too drunk, and you suck my cock very well. You are perfect in my books."

Brandon rolled on his side to face him and forced a smile. "Thanks," he said.

Dovzhenko slapped his rear affectionately. "It is time for you to go," he said. "Leave your number and I'll call you tomorrow to give you your reward."

The last thing Brandon wanted to do was encourage more contact, but he couldn't be sure his surreptitious recording had caught any information he and Troy could use. He picked up his jeans and took out his phone. "What's your number?" he asked. "I'll call you so I'll be in your phone."

"No," Dovzhenko said abruptly. "My number is private. You write yours down in the kitchen and I will call you."

Brandon acquiesced like it was a normal request. He dressed hurriedly and went in to write down his number on a small notepad he found.

"You need a ride?" Dovzhenko called after him. "I can have one of my men drive you wherever you need to go."

"No, it's fine, I can order one," said Brandon. "Thanks though."

Dovzhenko emerged from the bedroom unselfconsciously naked, holding a money clip. "You are such an easy boy to take care of," he said, pleased. "But I insist on at least paying for your ride." He peeled off a hundred-dollar bill and thrust it at Brandon, who thought it wise not to argue. He took the money and stuffed it into his front jeans pocket with a thank-you.

"I will speak to you tomorrow," Dovzhenko stated firmly.

"OK," Brandon said, then tried to inject more enthusiasm into his manner. "Looking forward to it," he added. Dovzhenko nodded, smirking, and walked him to the door of the apartment.

"Until tomorrow," he said.

"Right, bye," Brandon answered.

"Goodnight." With that Dovzhenko closed the door and Brandon was left standing in the hallway alone.

He quickly pressed the down button on the elevator and took it to the street level. He wasn't able to get a signal to call Troy until he was out in the lobby of the building. Troy picked up almost immediately.

"Yeah?" he asked.

"I'm leaving now," Brandon said quietly, pushing through the front door, overcome with relief at hearing his voice. "I'm outside the building. Can you come get me?"

# CHAPTER TWENTY-ONE

"Go around the block to your left and I'll be there in two seconds," Troy said and hung up. Brandon hurried down the street and turned the corner, and saw his car already waiting for him. He got in and Troy sped off.

"I didn't want to pull up front in case anyone was watching from the lobby," Troy explained.

"I get it," Brandon said, head lolling exhaustedly against the seat.

Troy looked at him with concern. "Are you OK? Did anything happen?"

Brandon laughed bitterly. "Oh yeah," he said. "I need to get home and shower."

* * *

Troy was mercifully silent on the car ride to Brandon's house, though he stole many glances at him. He followed Brandon in. "You need anything? Glass of water?"

Brandon shook his head. "Let me just jump in the shower real quick. I'll be right out."

He stood under the hot water for longer than he'd intended, scrubbing his body and washing his hair, and then lingering a while after that. Then he gargled thoroughly with mouthwash. He used the time to calm himself so he'd be able to talk normally to Troy. He didn't want to dwell on how the events of the evening had made him feel.

He put on sweats and a T-shirt, then went into the living room where Troy was sitting in the armchair, holding a beer and trying to look unconcerned, though Brandon saw his watchfulness.

Brandon sat on the couch. He found it hard to look Troy in the eye.

"Want to tell me what happened?" Troy nudged gently after some silence.

"Yeah," Brandon said, trying to sound nonchalant. "It went pretty well, I guess. I didn't find out much, but I did record part of a phone conversation he was having. He wasn't speaking English, but maybe we can get something from that."

"That's great!" Troy said. "I can get the file over to somebody who can enhance the sound and get it translated for us."

"Good," Brandon said tiredly.

"Anything else?"

Brandon described the group of men who worked for him, how Dovzhenko appeared to have a second apartment next door to his where possibly some of the men stayed. He told Troy what little Dovzhenko had said about his business activities. "That's about it," Brandon said. "But he wants to see me again tomorrow, so I can keep trying to find out more."

Troy saw the badly concealed dismay on Brandon's face. "Let me make some calls tonight," he said, "and see how fast we can get this recording processed. We'll see if it tells us anything before you go any farther."

"I'm fine," Brandon lied. "It was no big deal, really."

"Did you—did he—?"

"Yeah," Brandon said flatly. "I don't feel like talking about it, but it went fine."

Troy moved over to the couch. He touched Brandon's shoulder but felt him tense up and shrink away slightly at first. Troy slid his arms around Brandon's waist from behind, gently so he could pull away if he needed to. After some hesitation, Brandon relaxed against Troy's chest, closing his eyes and inhaling his cologne's scent, surprised again at how familiar and comforting it was after only a couple days. The two men sat silently like that for a while. Then Troy just as gently disengaged and asked to hear the recording on Brandon's phone.

* * *

As Troy made calls, Brandon lay on the couch, half-dozing but not wanting to be alone in his room.

Troy put down his phone. "We'll hopefully hear back tomorrow morning," he said. "I owe some favors, but they said they'd get it done as fast as they could."

He held out his hand, helped Brandon to his feet, and led him to his bedroom. Brandon lay on the bed, curled up slightly. "Do you want me to stay?" Troy asked. "Not to do anything," he quickly reassured him, "just to keep you company."

Brandon hesitated, then said, "Yeah."

Troy got into bed with him, still fully clothed. After a moment he moved onto his side and drew Brandon close against him with one arm. Brandon relaxed into him again, half asleep, imagining he was being shielded from memories of the night's events. Troy held him protectively as Brandon fell into a deeper slumber and the sky outside began to slowly get lighter.

* * *

Brandon woke alone in his bed after a few hours of deep sleep, the sheltering warmth of Troy's body having disappeared at some point while he slept. He went into the living room to see Troy pacing the floor, reading something on his phone.

Troy looked up when he noticed him enter. "Brandon, you did it!" he exclaimed.

"Did what?" Brandon said blearily.

"I got the translation back," Troy said, vibrating with excitement. He glanced back at his phone. "Dovzhenko says yes, the product will ship out tomorrow night—that means tonight—he even gives a port number! He says he wants to meet whoever he's speaking with to go over the details in the morning to make sure everything goes as planned. He says meet at the warehouse where the goods are stored." He looked at Brandon, his eyes glinting with excitement.

"What's it mean?" Brandon wondered aloud, sleep still clearing from his head.

"It could mean people," Troy said urgently. "He could be going to a warehouse where he keeps them. Shipping product—he could be sending some of them to a different place—or to another country. Traffickers like to move their captives from place to place to keep them disoriented." He took a couple of rapid breaths. "And if there's a place set up to keep people prisoner, well—" he hesitated as if afraid to say the next words "—if he's got Nasreen somewhere, it could be there!"

Brandon's heart began to race. He was fully awake now. "You think it's possible?" he asked, hardly daring to believe his ears.

Troy nodded. "I don't know how likely it is, but yes, I think it's possible." He spoke more firmly. "And that's what we have to focus on— the chance that she's alive. We can't spend time freaking out about the other possibilities." He gripped Brandon's shoulders. "OK?"

Brandon returned his nod, heart in his mouth. Troy pulled him into a hard hug.

"You did it," he said again, quietly this time.

Brandon's body slumped. He almost started crying but restrained himself. He couldn't define what he felt—relief, fear, hope—but it was intense.

"All right," he said, thinking about it more rationally. "OK, so how do we find the warehouse?"

"Well, we know he's going there sometime today, so I could stake out his apartment, now that we know where *that* is …"

Just then Brandon's phone buzzed on the coffee table. He picked it up and looked. "Unknown" was all it said on the screen, no incoming number. His eyes widened. "I think it's him."

# CHAPTER TWENTY-TWO

They both stared at the phone for a second. "He might want to see me," Brandon said, whispering for no reason.

"That could work," Troy said hastily. "That could help us figure out when he's going to his meeting. Answer it!"

Brandon accepted the call right before he would've missed it. "Hello?"

"Is this my pretty boy?" a man's voice with a slight but unmistakable accent said into his ear.

Brandon felt his face grow hot; he glanced at Troy and instinctively moved away from him. "Uh, maybe; is this Demi?"

Dovzhenko chuckled confidingly into his ear. "Of course," he said. "I hope you don't have too many men calling you to keep us straight."

"No, no," Brandon said, forcing a laugh, "not at all."

"Good," Dovzhenko said smugly. "Well, I want to meet you today and buy you something nice for being such a good boy, OK?"

"Um, uh, sure—yeah, that'd be great," Brandon fumbled. "I'm ready anytime." He looked over at Troy for confirmation that he was saying the right thing, and the man nodded slightly, hanging on every word of Brandon's side of the conversation.

"Great," Dovzhenko purred. "I'm glad it's not too early in the morning; I was afraid you'd be still in bed, all tired out."

"No, I'm OK," Brandon said, then lowered his voice and ad-libbed. "You wore me out, though, last night." He blushed knowing Troy heard him say it, but knew it was the right thing to say when he heard Dovzhenko's delighted laughter.

"Ah, my poor boy," he said. "I'll make it up to you today, OK?"

"You don't have to—I loved it," Brandon said, laying on the flattery as thick as he thought would be believable. "But I *would* like to see you again."

"Very good," Dovzhenko said. "Where should I send a car to get you?"

Brandon panicked and hit the mute button on his phone. "He's sending someone to get me," he hissed to Troy. "I shouldn't give him my address, should I?"

Troy shook his head vigorously. "Coffee shop," he suggested in a whisper. Brandon caught on, nodded and pushed unmute just as Dovzhenko said, "Are you there?"

"Oh good, you're back," Brandon said. "You cut out for a second. What'd you say?"

Dovzhenko repeated his request for his address, and Brandon told him he was just on his way to get some coffee. "Can you pick me up from the Space Roast coffee shop instead?" he asked. He gave Dovzhenko the cross streets of the nearby cafe and was told that a car would be there in fifteen minutes.

"We have no time to lose because I have some business to attend to and will need to send you away, sadly, at around ten-thirty," Dovzhenko said. "It's the only free time I will have today, so I wanted to use it to see you."

"I'm glad you're making time for me," Brandon said. "See you soon!" He hung up and quickly filled Troy in on the details.

"OK," Troy said. "Assuming he hasn't had his meeting yet, ten-thirty is probably when he needs to head over to the warehouse."

They hastily threw together a plan while Brandon threw fresh clothes on, glad he'd showered the night before. He brushed his teeth and they raced out to the car, where Troy got in the driver's seat and dropped him off at Space Roast.

He'd just gotten his cup of coffee and was turning away from the counter when he saw a black SUV pull up outside. He went outside just as a man with unmistakably Eastern European features stepped out of the driver's side.

"Are you from Dmytro?" Brandon asked innocuously.

"You're Brandon?" the man responded.

"That's right."

The man opened the back door and held it while Brandon got in. Something about the gesture triggered a sense of déjà vu, but he couldn't put his finger on it.

He belted himself in and was whisked away to Dovzhenko's high-rise. The man accompanied him up to the thirtieth floor, then asked him politely if he'd mind being patted down. Apparently Brandon's status had risen slightly already. He consented and got a considerably gentler frisking than the night before.

The man straightened after patting his ankles, a thoughtful expression on his face. "You look familiar to me," he mused.

Suddenly Brandon realized why his holding the car door had jogged his memory—the night of Nasreen's disappearance. He could see the man's face staring at him through the window after he'd ushered her into the back seat. Brandon's eyesight dimmed for a second as pure panic rushed through him.

"You hang out at Purgatory a lot?" the driver asked, and Brandon grasped at that.

"Pretty often," he said. "Maybe that's it."

"Yeah," the man said slowly. "Must be." He knocked at Dovzhenko's door, and the man himself answered it wearing a dressing gown.

"Ah, Brandon!" he exclaimed with genuine pleasure, and despite himself, Brandon almost felt a twinge of guilt at leading him on.

"Thank you Yevhen, you can go," Dovzhenko said to the driver, and added a few terse words in Ukrainian. The man nodded and headed back to the elevator.

Dovzhenko turned to Brandon, beaming. "I'll call for Yevhen soon to come take us for a quick shopping trip," he said. "I wanted to have you all to myself first, though." He stepped back and waved Brandon in.

The younger man's heart sank; he'd been hoping this would be solely a public date, but apparently he wouldn't get away unscathed. He steeled himself and walked past Dovzhenko into his apartment.

Dovzhenko closed the door and came over to him, holding out his arms. Brandon embraced the shorter, stockier man, feeling Dovzhenko's hands trail down to fondle his ass. "How are you feeling?" the man asked with joking sympathy as he squeezed.

"Pretty sore," Brandon admitted. It was the truth, but he said it because he got the sense Dovzhenko liked feeling powerful.

"You look so strong yet you are so delicate," Dovzhenko teased. "Don't worry, I will give you time to heal today." He settled on the couch and gestured pointedly at the floor in front of him. Brandon got the message. Kneeling, he parted the folds of the dressing gown and worked as efficiently as possible.

As Dovzhenko neared climax, he put a hand on Brandon's head and held him there. "Drink it all," he said in a guttural voice. Brandon fought back his gag reflex and swallowed hastily.

Dovzhenko sighed with satisfaction. "Now I am going to have to buy you even more nice things," he said as Brandon stood up and wiped his mouth on the back of his arm. "Wait while I get dressed and we can go."

Minutes later, Yevhen knocked on the door to bring them down to the car. Brandon tried to stay turned away from the driver as much as possible without being obvious, so he'd have fewer opportunities to study his face.

Dovzhenko had them driven to an upscale retail area. Brandon couldn't have been less interested in shopping, his mind full of thoughts about finding the warehouse and looking for Nasreen, but he didn't want to make the man suspicious. Dovzhenko insisted on buying him a leather jacket at an expensive department store. He also picked out a solid gold lighter. "What do you think of this?" he asked.

"It's really cool, but I don't smoke," Brandon said, realizing as he said it that he could have just thanked the man and taken the unwanted gift.

"Well, I enjoy a cigar from time to time, so you should have one around," Dovzhenko said regally, and added it to the purchase. Brandon didn't get a look at the price tags but blanched at the total. Dovzhenko made Brandon wear the jacket out of the store and tuck the lighter in the pocket of his jeans. Despite Brandon's discomfort, the clerk who rang them up never raised an eyebrow.

Then Dovzhenko took Brandon to a bar that served breakfast, and ordered him a champagne and a vodka for himself. As they drank, Dovzhenko grandly praised how the jacket looked on Brandon, preening with pride over his own generosity. Brandon tried to seem appropriately impressed and grateful, but his mind was miles away.

They only stayed for one drink. It was nearly ten-thirty. "Well, my pretty boy, I'm afraid I have to leave you here," he said. He stood and handed Brandon another hundred-dollar bill. "I need to take my car; will you be able to order your own?"

"Sure, no problem," Brandon said, but he was caught by surprise. He thought he'd have more time to alert Troy. "Uh, when will I see you again?"

Dovzhenko cupped Brandon's chin with one pudgy hand and ran his thumb suggestively over the younger man's lips. "Soon, baby, soon," he said soothingly. "I am already hungry for you again, but I must go. And you need to rest up for me." He leaned down and kissed Brandon's lips for the first time, then snapped his fingers for the waiter. "One more glass of champagne for my young friend, and take this to cover the bill." He passed a hundred to the server, whose eyes widened slightly; their drinks had come to perhaps fifty.

Dovzhenko left in a marvelous mood, while Brandon frantically got out his phone and started texting Troy. "Hes on the move now," he wrote, "leaving from 7th & pine." Brandon looked out the window and saw Dovzhenko just getting into the back of the car. Yevhen shut the door for him and went around to the driver side. He took a moment to wipe a spot on the windshield with his sleeve.

Brandon got a text back. "Can u stall him 2 mins," it read.

# CHAPTER TWENTY-THREE

He leapt up from the table and ran outside just as Yevhen was getting in. "Wait!" he said. He knocked on Dovzhenko's tinted window and, after a moment, it rolled down. He took his new lighter out. "Need a light?" he asked. The older man looked quizzically at him. Brandon tried for a charming smile and reached in to stroke Dovzhenko's cheek.

"Actually, I really just wanted to say I'll miss you," he said, looking deep into the man's eyes.

Dovzhenko recovered from his surprise and chuckled. "I should always feed you champagne in the morning," he said. "You're not quite so shy and quiet all of a sudden."

Brandon leaned in and kissed Dovzhenko with all the feigned passion he could muster, making it last as long as he could. Finally the man put his hand on Brandon's chest and pushed him playfully away. "All right, I've really got to go now, you troublemaker," he said affectionately. "I'll call you soon." Brandon pulled back as if with reluctance and stood with his hands in the pockets of his new leather jacket as Dovzhenko's window hummed closed again.

He watched the car pull away and go a couple of blocks before the left turn signal came on. He got out his phone again and texted "going left on 5th" to Troy. "black suv" he added.

He lost sight of them and waited breathlessly for a response. It was minutes later but felt like much more when his phone buzzed again. "got em" was all it said. Brandon's body filled with exultation.

* * *

Troy followed the SUV a few cars behind in Brandon's car. His breakneck race through the city had panned out; he'd caught sight of them pulling onto an entrance ramp just in time. He was on their tail as they exited the highway and headed down an access road.

He'd hoped to have time to pick Brandon up and take advantage of his familiarity with the city, but the turn of events meant he'd have to go it alone. As long as he kept sight of the black car, they hadn't blown their chance to discover the location of the warehouse. He thought admiringly of the way Brandon had stepped up to the plate in their mission, and of the unexpected way they'd bonded.

He'd never really gotten to know anyone Nasreen had dated before. They only saw other people when they were apart, and things had always stayed casual with everyone except each other. The thought of being jealous never occurred to him; if anything, he was pleased that others got to experience Nasreen's magic.

He never questioned whether she loved him as much as he did her.

When they were together, they fit together so seamlessly that sometimes he felt almost like they were one person. It was one reason he did have hope she could be alive. He knew what he'd do, and so he felt confident she'd be using every scrap of her considerable strength—outer and inner—and cunning to survive whatever situation she was in.

With Brandon, Troy had been skeptical of his usefulness at first but reluctantly charmed by his sincerity and determination. He was honestly surprised how quickly he'd gone from viewing Nasreen's lover as somewhat of an expendable—if headily attractive—resource to genuinely caring about him and feeling protective of him. He felt a sickening pang of guilt thinking of the night before. It had been hard to watch him get into Dovzhenko's car that night, and even harder to hide the depth of his concern at seeing Brandon so visibly shaken when he'd picked him up afterward.

It was painful to think of Brandon putting himself in the hands of the very man who might have taken Nasreen. Troy remembered longingly the night in the hotel, exploring Brandon's lean body and beautifully shaped lips. Initiating that had been an impulsive move on his part; he'd sensed a conflicted sort of attraction in Brandon that he couldn't resist testing.

Maybe, too, he'd been curious to touch someone Nasreen had been with. Either way, he'd decided on a whim to see how far he could go before the man showed discomfort, expecting to tease him a little before Brandon got too freaked out and he backed off. He'd been stunned at how deeply Brandon allowed himself to be immersed in the experience, especially considering it was clearly his first time. And at how intensely exciting it was to seduce him. Even now his pulse raced as he remembered.

Since then it had been nearly impossible to look at Brandon without thinking about that night. He exercised every ounce of restraint not to let on, though sometimes touching Brandon was irresistible. He thought of the trusting way he melted into Troy every time he held him. Then he shook himself back to reality before he completely lost himself in fantasies.

He followed the SUV around several turns and into an industrial-looking area. The vehicle slowed, and Troy pulled in behind an ancient pickup truck parked on the side of the street. From there he could see the men get out in front of a square brick building about five stories high. Dovzhenko's driver spoke on his phone, and a large garage-style door raised open. Troy thought he glimpsed a man with a machine gun standing in the gloom inside, but he couldn't be sure.

Dovzhenko and his driver disappeared inside, the door lowered, and Troy got out of Brandon's car. He hurried around the sides of the building, assessing it for possible entrance points.

All the windows were reinforced with steel bars. But on one side he spotted an old-fashioned fire escape that started one floor up.

Troy looked around; seeing no one, he jumped for the ladder, but it was at least a couple feet out of reach. He went around to the back of the building and found a plastic garbage bin on wheels. He tilted it and rolled it as quietly as he could around the corner and under the fire escape.

After several tries, wincing every time it started to tip and then landed loudly upright, he scrambled on top of the lid. Once he steadied himself, he knelt up and slowly reached his hands above his head. He stretched, afraid to look up for fear of losing his balance. At last he felt his fingers brush against rusty metal and grasped the edge. The ladder came down and he clung to it, his feet slipping off the trash can lid. The bin tipped over with a loud clatter, but he managed to hold onto the ladder and clamber up to the first level of the fire escape.

He crouched there for a minute or two, listening for voices, doors, or any other signs that someone had heard the trash can fall. When no one appeared, he climbed up the stairs to the top landing. Another ladder extended upward to the roof. He scaled it and clambered on top of the building.

He surveyed the roof and again saw no one guarding it. He crept to a door and tried it. Locked, of course, but it was just a simple door lock and not a deadbolt. He pulled out a pocketknife and inserted the blade behind the lock, pulling until it clicked open.

He opened the door cautiously, making sure no alarm sounded, and stole down a short steep flight of stairs. He found himself in a hallway dimly lit by greenish fluorescent ceiling lights, which revealed dull concrete floors and exposed wood ceilings with ancient-looking pipes running along them. A faint but distinct odor of urine permeated the air.

The hallway was lined with battered but sturdy-looking metal doors at regular intervals. Each door had a small glass pane reinforced by crisscrossing wires, but when he peered into the one nearest him, all he saw was darkness. He pressed his ear to it but couldn't hear anything, and wondered if it was soundproof.

He couldn't tell if anything or anyone was inside.

He heard a door swing open somewhere down the hall and ducked back into the stairwell he'd just come out of. Male voices grew louder as they got closer. He pressed himself against the wall of the stairwell and listened, but they were speaking another language.

He heard a door near him clang open, and one of the men barked orders—to his companion, or to someone in the room, he couldn't be sure.

Then Troy heard a muffled female voice, weak, pleading. He couldn't tell what language was being spoken or how old the person was— she could've been a girl or a grown woman. One of the men spat some words and the female voice cried out sharply as if whoever it was had been struck.

Troy tensed, holding himself back from his instinct to try and intervene. He wasn't sure how many men there were. He thought he'd heard two, but if there were more and he tried to attack, one of them might be able to get away and raise the alarm.

The door banged shut and the men's footsteps and voices went the other way. Troy peered out in time to see them round the corner out of sight.

He sidled down the hallway, clinging to the wall, and turned the corner. A door at the end of that hallway looked different from the others. He opened it to a stairwell that led down a level.

As he neared the next landing, he heard more conversation. This time, one of the men sounded American, and the others were speaking accented English.

"Yes, tonight's shipment still has capacity," one of the Ukrainian men said. "So anyone who has given trouble, who is not cooperating, this is time to gather them up and—" he made a whistling noise. "Hopefully they learn lesson by the time they get to Dubai." He laughed. "This is Last Chance Express for them." The other men joined in his laughter.

"So anyway, bring 'em to the holding pen by eleven," the American said. "The ship leaves at midnight and we load them in last thing before it goes. Make sure you dope 'em up good before you bring 'em down; they need to be real quiet."

"And record them properly," another man said. "We need roll call before the ship leaves, and it needs to match. Boss doesn't want any screw-ups, especially with that fed bitch. She's why he's here in person."

"Yeah, we need to do this one just right. Diavol is watching it," the American concurred.

The voices started to fade as they went down the hall. "Oh, and we need to clear out room for another group coming in two days. See if we can pack some of the upstairs cages tighter tomorrow, OK?"

Troy stood frozen, replaying what he thought he'd heard. "Fed bitch." Was he imagining things? It could have been something entirely different. If Dovzhenko was trying to rid himself of an intrusive agent, would he really try to sell her on the black market? It seemed extremely risky. But so was running a criminal operation while being an ambassador.

He had to get to the "holding pen." He descended two more flights of stairs.

The main floor of the warehouse was bustling. Troy peered out of the stairwell as men carted crates of what looked like packaged food and drink supplies, conferred over clipboards and half-packed boxes, serviced a truck parked inside the giant open area, stood at the ready with machine guns.

In the middle of it all stood Dovzhenko, talking to three men. Although Troy couldn't hear what they were saying, he saw that the other men seemed both alert and deferential. The rest of the action swirled around the small group, giving them a wide berth.

Troy remained in his spot, trying to make out what Dovzhenko was saying, but his voice was no more than a murmur within the hubbub. He might not have been speaking English anyway.

Then a new sound came, a protesting creaking sound like a gate being opened. Troy inched forward to look out again. Most of the men in the room were looking toward giant metal plates that someone was hauling a pulley to move. The huge panels moved outward, revealing a chain-link enclosure about twenty feet wide and possibly that deep. It was difficult to gauge because it was so tightly packed.

Inside were at least fifty people, mostly women and girls, though Troy saw a few young men and boys as well. Most were sitting or lying on the bare concrete floor. Almost all of them appeared to be heavily sedated or on drugs, or maybe just too weakened or defeated to react much when the metal panels were removed. Several squinted as if unused to light.

Dovzhenko moved toward the enclosure, and the men around him quieted. He paused, surveying the tableau of human misery before him. Then he moved closer to one end, the side farthest from Troy's vantage point.

Troy saw he was fixated on one figure, a woman slumped against one of the chain-link sides, her arms folded around her bent knees. She seemed to be wearing a short tight dress that at some point could have been expensive and chic, though the dark material was torn and dusty. She was barefoot. Dovzhenko turned back to the men, pointing at her, and said something questioning. One of them nodded. He looked around and picked up a long rod lying on the floor and pushed it through the chain-links, prodding the slumped woman.

Slowly she raised her head. Troy gasped.

# CHAPTER TWENTY-FOUR

Nasreen had dark circles under her eyes, and her full lips were dry and painfully cracked. Her hair, slightly longer than chin length, looked dirty, hanging around her face in greasy clumps. Despite all of that, it was clear she was a striking beauty.

Though she looked sedated and weak like the other prisoners, she stared straight at Dovzhenko, and Troy thought there was some level of alertness, even defiance, in her eyes.

Her gaze slid past Dovzhenko as if dismissing him. She squinted, blinked, and then her eyes flared with recognition. Troy's heart caught in his throat. She was looking directly at him.

Troy froze for a second, then ducked back into the stairwell. It was too uncanny, too direct, her stare—he felt sure Dovzhenko's men would start turning to see what she was looking at so intently.

He felt elated to see her alive—he'd had far more serious doubts than he'd ever let on to Brandon—but heartbroken at the condition she was in and the suffering she must be going through, and terrified at the seeming impossibility of her situation. This must be the "holding pen" of people being shipped out tonight—which gave him very little time to help.

He was tempted to peer out again, to see what else was happening. But there were no audible signs that he'd been spotted, and he heard the gates screeching closed again. Evidently Dovzhenko had just wanted to see for himself that Nasreen was where he wanted her to be.

Troy desperately wanted to stay and help her but, alone and armed only with a pocketknife, he knew he had virtually no chance of doing anything but getting them both killed. So instead he started up the stairs.

Rounding the corner to the second landing, he suddenly came face to face with another man. He didn't know how he hadn't heard him coming—he must've been too preoccupied to take the same amount of care he had on the way down the stairs. Troy froze, unsure whether to attack, run past him upstairs, or try to make a break for it back downstairs.

In that split second of indecision, the man nodded curtly and walked past him. Troy stared down after him, but the man didn't stop or look back. He'd simply assumed Troy worked there.

His limbs rubbery with relief, he climbed the rest of the way to the top floor, hurried down the green-hued hallway with the metal doors, and found his way back up to the roof. Then he climbed back down the ladder and fire escape. His garbage can was still on its side, but it was much easier to descend; he dropped from the ladder into the alley with no trouble.

Then he crept around the side of the building. Dovzhenko and his driver hadn't left yet; the SUV was still sitting parked outside. Troy took note of the cross streets the warehouse sat at the corner of, then hurried back to Brandon's car.

He texted with one hand while he hurtled north on the same road he'd taken to get to the warehouse. His first text simply said "shes alive"

A few moments later, before Brandon had even had a chance to respond, he sent a second one: "but in trouble"

* * *

Back at home, and with no one around to look strong for, Brandon sobbed as he read the two messages. First with relief and then with a combination of that and terror.

When he could breathe, he called Troy. "How can I help?"

He heard highway sounds as Troy paused. "Hang tight—I'll be there soon."

* * *

It was early afternoon when Troy returned to the house. Brandon was waiting for him at the door, wide-eyed and brimming with nerves. Troy related the morning's events to him, pacing restlessly the whole time.

Brandon tried to focus on how to move forward, but his brain kept coming back to the fact that Nasreen might have been in there, not more than thirty minutes away from his home, for weeks while he was moping outside her apartment. He listened to Troy's description of her with a terrible guilt. But he pushed those thoughts aside, no matter how many times they tried to intrude.

There was suddenly exponentially more hope, now that she was confirmed to be alive. There was also an excessive amount of risk and difficulty in saving her, and a very narrow window of time.

"What can we do?" Brandon asked. In his mind Troy was practically a superhero: climbing up the side of the building, breaking in, evading detection. It was so far beyond anything he himself could ever imagine doing.

But even Troy, he thought, wouldn't be able to defeat the legions of criminals working the warehouse for Dovzhenko. This was bigger than the two of them. He said it aloud.

Troy agreed.

* * *

They were seen almost immediately by Nasreen's liaison, Jeff Hanson, a friendly man with shaggy graying brown hair, glasses and a tall thin frame. His assistant, a burly younger man, introduced himself as Agent Koski and then attended the rest of the interview in silence.

Brandon let Troy do the talking; he felt he'd have a better sense of what parts of their story they shouldn't reveal—be able to gauge the severity of the various lines they'd crossed in the course of their private investigation.

He was right to trust Troy, who laid it out masterfully, not revealing all of their tactics but not directly lying about any of their actions either. He skimmed over most of the details, arriving quickly at the revelation that a shipment of human cargo would be leaving that night, with Nasreen included.

The agents listened with growing concern, taking furious notes. "My God!" Hanson exclaimed when it was over. "You're sure of this?"

Troy assured him he was. Hanson scrubbed at his face. "It wasn't unusual for Nasreen not to check in with me for long periods of time. I wasn't officially part of her investigation; I was just her local contact for anything she needed—information, manpower. She didn't need much—she was pretty self-sufficient. She reported back to Washington, and I have no idea how often they expected her to get in touch."

"It doesn't matter why it happened," Troy said with some impatience. "She's being taken away tonight! She needs your help *now*."

"Yes, yes, sorry," said Hanson. "There will be time to figure out what procedural changes can be made in the future to avoid something like this. The important thing is rescuing Nasreen—and putting a stop to this whole operation." He stood up and reached out to shake their hands. "I want to thank you men for what you did. Agent Hassan is one of our own, and we'll do everything in our power to secure her release, safe and sound."

The two men stood when Hanson did, but Brandon blurted, "We can help!"

Hanson smiled ruefully and spread his hands. "I'd love to take you up on that, believe me. But the FBI has very strict protocol, and now that this is in our hands, we can't let civilians get involved." He clapped Brandon on the back with confidence. "Don't worry; you've done the right thing by bringing this to our attention. We won't waste any time putting a rescue mission together." He looked gravely at them. "Now I want you both to stay far away from these people and that warehouse. I don't want you in danger, and I also can't have you interfering with the FBI mission. Lives are at stake here."

He led them out of his office and to the front door, where he shook their hands and thanked them again. Troy didn't protest, so Brandon followed his lead and they left the building.

They got in the car and Brandon drove away, glancing over at Troy in the passenger seat. The other man seemed preoccupied, staring at his hands or occasionally closing his eyes and pinching the bridge of his nose with his fingers. Brandon let him have as long as he needed.

Finally Troy looked over at him. "We're not staying away," he said.

# CHAPTER TWENTY-FIVE

Brandon exhaled forcefully as if he'd been holding his breath. "OK," he said with a mixture of relief and dread. "What do you think we should do?"

"Not sure yet," Troy said. "But we're not just handing this over. The FBI is just like the Marines, just like any job—most people are really good at what they do but others just aren't. We can't take a chance on which kind are working on this mission." He laughed humorlessly. "I mean, think about it. Without us, no one would even know she was missing. I don't think anyone was trying to find her except you and me."

* * *

They gathered supplies and went to the warehouse. Troy found a way up a neighboring building and helped Brandon ascend to the roof, equipped with a pair of binoculars and food and drink so he could stay up there all day. Troy parked a couple blocks away, out of sight behind another car. This time he'd brought a gun.

They'd agreed that they shouldn't actively interfere with the FBI. They'd simply watch. If anything went wrong, Troy would go in and try to extract Nasreen. It was still early in the evening; they settled in for a long wait.

* * *

She no longer even noticed the smell of the unwashed bodies around her, or the filthiness of the gritty concrete floor. Nasreen sat slumped over as if half-unconscious, propped against the fence that imprisoned her.

Her arms appeared to hang limply, but one hand was concealed from sight by her hip, gradually grinding a pill into dust by rubbing it against the floor with minute movements.

When she'd first been taken, the tranquilizers had been administered intravenously and she'd had no way to avoid them. She'd drifted in and out of consciousness, sometimes waking enough to eat stale crackers and tepid water, or whatever subsistence fare was given to her. Sometimes she woke to find various men, pants lowered to just below their hips, grinding on top of her, sometimes tugging the straps of her dress down to expose and grope her breasts. She couldn't feel much of anything and lay passively until it was over.

Then they changed to pills. She wasn't sure if they'd run out of the intravenous kind or only used it in the initial stages when people would be more able to resist. Maybe they wanted the track marks to fade before they handed their prisoners over to whoever was buying them. For whatever reason, they started bringing pills and water. And she started hiding the pills under her tongue until they left, then spitting them out and pulverizing them. And her head started to clear.

She wasn't sure how long she'd been there by that point; time had seemed not to exist while she was under sedation. Once she had her wits about her, the days went by with agonizing slowness. She couldn't really talk to her fellow captives; not only were they too doped up and traumatized, but she didn't want to tip her hand and risk having her captors find out she was conscious.

Not resisting their assaults took an immense amount of willpower. She would observe her attackers' vulnerability as they took advantage of her, assuming she was drugged and demoralized. She would note the moments when she would easily have been able to snap their wrist, break their nose, punch their windpipe so they'd be gasping for breath for hours. It would be a temporary satisfaction followed by probably her torture or death, so she clung to the knowledge that she could have done it, and instead lay limply, pretending to be barely conscious.

She chose to continue her ruse in the hopes that fellow agents were coming to rescue her. She wasn't due to check in with D.C. for another month, but surely someone in Seattle would notice something was amiss. As the days dragged by, though, she wondered if they would, and what her kidnappers' end game was. Did they hope to collect a ransom? If they weren't intending to trade her for money, why were they keeping her alive?

It was only in the holding pen, when she started hearing whispers that they'd be sent somewhere soon, that her steadfast faith in her agency really started to falter, and that she realized why she hadn't been killed or ransomed. It was Diavol's sadistic revenge that she would suffer the same fate she had tried to rescue others from.

Still she continued to conceal and destroy her pills. She resolved to look for any conceivable avenue of escape, whether it happened here or in whatever her destination city or country was. It felt like a futile resolution, and her hope dimmed with each passing hour.

And then, without warning, her eyes fell on an unmistakable figure peering out from the shadows—Troy. Her Troy. She swore he met her gaze for a few seconds and then was gone.

After he disappeared, and the metal plates shuddered back into place, she did question what she'd seen. Maybe she wasn't as lucid as she'd assumed, and he'd been a figment of her imagination. But she became convinced it had been him. Maybe he'd come to her apartment, found it abandoned, and somehow put together the pieces of what had happened to her.

Until the abduction, she'd been counting down the days until she saw him again. In fact, his arrival had been on her mind moments before she'd been taken. It seemed a million years ago, yet wearing the same dress the entire time was a constant reminder of her date that night, the overwhelming happiness and worry that had preoccupied her so that she hadn't seen the gun trained on her until it was too late. Brandon, who was just meant to be an adorable pastime, had said he loved her. And she knew she was in deeper than she'd ever admitted to herself. Once she'd gotten past his tongue-tied awkwardness (and the stunning good looks he was seemingly unaware of), she'd found a thoughtful, curious man who cared deeply about his students and the world they were learning to navigate. And as their relationship had deepened, so had his self-confidence.

As she'd walked toward the street from the bar that last night, she'd been wondering if there could be a happy outcome for her and both men. Especially Brandon, who was still so naive in some ways. She'd dreaded telling him about Troy, something she'd initially thought they'd never get serious enough to discuss, and which had seemed harder to bring up with every passing day. But with Troy's imminent arrival, and with Brandon's declaration of love, she knew the moment of truth had arrived. At least until she saw the flash of a gun barrel and everything changed.

If Troy was there in Seattle, if she really had seen him, that meant she'd spent over two weeks in captivity; but how *much* longer? How long had he searched for her before he'd found the warehouse?

Another unanswered question was why *he* was there, not someone from the Bureau. Was he not in contact with them? If he'd been able to figure out where she was, why hadn't someone from her agency?

It didn't add up, but she felt confident that it had really been him and not a mirage. And the fact that *someone* now knew where she was told her that a rescue operation was probably in the works.

Still, with as much staff and firepower as Dovzhenko had on his side, it would be a difficult mission, and she knew there were a hundred ways it could go wrong. And was the Bureau even involved? Was Troy on his own for some reason? Whatever the answer, she felt she needed to be as alert as possible.

So she ground up her pills, and watched and waited. She didn't know what else she could do at the moment. It was better than nothing.

# CHAPTER TWENTY-SIX

The moments before the call were some of the happiest of Dovzhenko's life. And happiness was hard to come by when you were as powerful as he was, with enemies out to thwart him and even those who worked for him threatening to bring him down with their sheer incompetence. Nevertheless, as always, he'd managed to handle everything that was thrown at him and come out on top. He lounged on his sofa, finger circling the rim of his glass, eyes glazed over as he savored his triumphs.

The bitch was going to suffer like nothing she could imagine—what she was currently experiencing didn't even compare. That thought alone would've made him hard, if he hadn't already been reliving what had taken place within the past twenty-four hours on this very couch.

If he had one gripe about his gorgeous new plaything, it was that he was perhaps *too* compliant. He liked there to be a little friction, a little struggle before he brought them to that state. Still, Brandon would slip up and do something to displease him. Dovzhenko was sure of it, and thought dreamily of how he would correct him, lovingly but firmly. Maybe it would happen tomorrow, when he was celebrating the bitch's safe transport to her own personal hell. Maybe not for a few weeks. Yes, it would be even sweeter if he let Brandon get complacent, attached, a little spoiled, before bringing him to heel.

Dovzhenko licked his lips imagining various ways the scene could play out. His hand strayed to his lap and unfastened his pants. But he'd barely gotten started when his phone rang.

He sighed and reluctantly withdrew his hand to pick it up. His eyes narrowed when he saw who it was.

"What is it?" he barked impatiently.

He was mostly silent during the rest of the call. His erection faded, forgotten.

After he hung up, he zipped his trousers and stood, walking calmly into the kitchen and setting down his glass. Then he pounded the counter with all his strength, until he had to stop and clutch his fist with his other hand, breathing heavily with pain and anger. He stayed where he was, eyes closed, until his breath steadied. He took out his phone and held it to his ear. No one picked up and he cut off the voicemail message as soon as it began, letting loose a string of profanities in Ukrainian.

He hit another number in his contacts. "Yevhen. Come." He gritted his teeth so hard he could barely get words out. *"Now."*

# CHAPTER TWENTY-SEVEN

On the roof of the building next to the warehouse, Brandon felt his phone vibrate. He pulled it out and saw "Unknown" on the screen.

Heart in mouth, he hesitated. He hadn't been expecting to hear from Dovzhenko so soon. In fact he'd thought, perhaps naively, that the man would be taken into custody today and he'd never hear from him again.

He let the call go to his voicemail and texted Troy. "D just tried to call. shd i take it if he calls back"

His phone buzzed. "no dont. u dont need 2 see him again"

Brandon breathed a sigh of relief. His phone received one more call from "Unknown," but he ignored it and it stopped ringing. No voicemails were left, which he thought a bit strange, but maybe the man was equally as secretive about leaving recordings of his voice as he was about giving out his number. That made Brandon smile with triumph at the thought of the recording *he'd* made. He put his phone in his pocket and went back to his surveillance.

The area had been quiet for the two or so hours he and Troy had been staking it out. A few cars went by without stopping, but it was an abnormally deserted area compared with usual city traffic.

As the sun started to set, a box truck pulled up to the building. Brandon put his binoculars to his eyes. As he watched, the large garage-style door was hoisted open and the truck drove inside. He caught sight of armed men inside the cavernous-looking first-floor room before the door lowered again and shut with a clang he could hear from his rooftop perch.

He texted Troy: "truck went in bldg"

Troy replied: "prob getting ready for 2nite"

Just then a black SUV pulled up to the warehouse. Brandon instinctively ducked his head a couple inches when he saw Yevhen, his driver from that morning, get out with his phone pressed to his ear. Another man in the passenger seat stayed in the car.

The building door opened again and he walked inside.

Another plain white truck drove up and parked in front of the warehouse behind Yevhen's vehicle. Brandon watched for a while, but the door didn't open for it. That truck remained where it was with the driver inside.

After fifteen minutes, the door moved upward again. But this time it was letting a vehicle out—the first box truck. It rumbled down the street, and the second one pulled in.

Brandon called Troy. He couldn't explain the whole situation via text.

"Yeah?"

"I think they're moving people out. Did you see the truck that just left? Why would they do that now?"

"I don't know, but I guess I'd better try to follow them," Troy said tensely. "Hang on." Brandon heard the screech of tires as Troy pulled out, and he could see his car, a couple blocks down, take the same turn as the first box truck.

"I'm climbing down," Brandon said. "I won't be able to do anything from up here."

"OK, but be careful," Troy said.

"I'll call you when I get to the street," Brandon said and hung up.

He went to the side of the building with the fire escape that Troy had helped him onto and climbed carefully. He dropped to the ground and stole quietly around the building toward the alley between his building and the warehouse.

He heard the door opening upward again as he came down the alley toward the front of the buildings. He was right by a plastic trash bin that had tipped on its side, and he crouched as low as he could behind it.

The second truck exited the building, and he saw that a third had pulled up. It rolled in once the second one was clear of the entrance.

The second truck drove out of sight, and Brandon pulled out his phone. Troy picked up almost immediately. "They're taking more people out," he whispered. "Three trucks so far. What should I do?"

Troy swore. "This one I'm following isn't going toward the port," he said. "We're going farther inland. Something's happening."

"How do we know which truck has Nasreen?" Brandon asked.

"I don't know." Troy was silent for a tense moment. "Fuck!"

"Well," Brandon said, hesitantly, "keep following that truck so we at least know where they're going. Hopefully if they're moving everyone, they'll take Nasreen there too."

"OK," Troy said. "What about you?"

"I don't—" he stopped as he saw a fourth truck pull up. The building door creaked up again. "I'll call you back." He clicked the phone off and watched.

Instead of the third truck leaving the garage, he saw a man exiting on foot. As he heard the door clatter back down, he realized it was Yevhen. He was shepherding another person, clearly a woman, with a black shapeless hood covering her entire head. Her hands were bound behind her back and she was barefoot.

# CHAPTER TWENTY-EIGHT

It took Brandon several seconds to process what he saw: the woman's black dress, torn and misshapen, still had glints of silver shining through the dust and grime that coated it.

His ears were ringing and his vision became tunnel-like so he could see only her and Yevhen. Nasreen stumbled blindly, her feet moving tentatively, and Yevhen hauled her up roughly before she could fall completely. Brandon's heart wrenched and he nearly cried out, wanting to run forward. But he stopped himself. Shaking his head to try and clear it, he looked desperately around for some kind of weapon. He saw a piece of metal that might have been part of a storage shelf; it had holes drilled through it at regular intervals. He picked it up just in time to see Yevhen pushing Nasreen to the floor of the SUV's back seat, then quickly tying her ankles together with a short length of cord. The car's other occupant watched. Probably armed; Brandon stayed put. Yevhen slammed the door, hurried around to the driver side, got in and took off.

Brandon bit his lip again to keep from making a sound and crept forward, peering out to see if anyone else was outside the building. There was only the driver sitting in the fourth box truck, idling at the curb. The truck faced away from Brandon, and he came toward it, bent low, hoping the man wouldn't look in his side mirror. But he was watching the front of the building and didn't see Brandon, who reached his driver side door, took a deep breath, and reached up and grabbed at the handle, pulling with all his strength.

The door flew open and the driver, who must have been leaning on it slightly, started to fall. The man's flailing hands managed to grip the sides of the truck and prevent him from falling headfirst out of the vehicle.

Brandon had stepped back instinctively when it seemed the driver would tumble straight down onto him. When he realized the man had righted himself, but was still scrambling to stand up and turn, he raised the metal bar over his head and brought it down on the driver's skull as hard as he could.

He wasn't prepared for what he saw. The man's dark hair parted like split pants, revealing a raw, angry strip of red from which blood gushed out.

The driver did fall to the pavement this time, losing his grip, and Brandon stepped aside. Then, as the wounded man clutched his head, groaning, trying to get to his feet, Brandon jumped over him and into the front seat of the truck.

The keys were in the ignition, engine running, so Brandon slammed his foot on the unfamiliar clutch and put it in drive using the large stick shift. He tried to make a U-turn but had to back up once to complete it. By then the driver had staggered upright, his now-bloody hands still pressed to his head, and stumbled toward the truck, yelling incoherently. Brandon threw the truck back into drive and gunned the accelerator, peeling off.

He sped toward the access road, thinking that might be what Yevhen took to get wherever he was going. Sure enough, he saw the familiar black SUV just entering it. Brandon followed as closely as he dared. He thought the truck he was driving was generic enough in appearance that it wouldn't rouse suspicion, but he tried to keep a small distance between them just in case.

They took the access road onto the highway. Yevhen was going about the speed limit, so Brandon found it easy to keep up with him. He must not have realized he was being followed, Brandon decided. He noticed only then that there was a firearm on the seat next to him, a long gun … maybe a rifle. He'd never had any interest in guns so had never learned any of the terminology.

Once they were on the relatively straight highway, Brandon called Troy and quickly caught him up on the situation.

"Holy shit!" Troy said. "That's—incredible." Brandon felt a surge of adrenaline-fueled pride despite his fear. "I saw where they brought the first truck; it went into another warehouse about fifteen minutes east of the other one. I'll call Hanson and give him the address. And I'll let him know we're tracking where Nasreen's being taken. I'm gonna try to catch up with you." Earlier they'd installed a GPS app on their phones so they could find one another if needed. Troy activated it and got directions. "I'll let you know when I'm on the highway. Call me when they turn off, OK?"

"Got it," Brandon said. He hung up, eyes glued to the black SUV.

He followed it for forty-five minutes to an hour before it exited onto a two-lane highway. It was getting dark by now, but there was no one else on the road, so it was easy to keep track of. He called Troy Sand let him know the exit number. "Yep, I'm only a few miles behind you," Troy said. "Maybe you should stay on the line with me."

Brandon did, and let Troy know each turn they made. Between him giving directions, they speculated where they could be heading. "Why did the plan change?" Troy said. "Why'd they pull her out and take her somewhere different from the others?"

Brandon searched his mind for possible answers. "Well, what if—if the situation changed?" he asked lamely. "Something that made it impossible to ship out tonight?"

"Right, and they separated Nasreen because of something they found out about her?"

"Yeah, so they already knew she was FBI, obviously. Maybe they decided they should try and use her for something else."

"Could be," Troy said musingly. They drove in silence, mulling that over.

By then they'd made several more turns. Troy was gaining but still out of sight. Brandon slowed to increase the distance between him and the SUV, keenly aware that they were the only two vehicles in sight on the narrow, winding two-lane road. He hoped Yevhen hadn't grown suspicious of the truck that seemed to be going the exact same way as him.

The SUV slowed and made a hard right onto a small path that appeared to go straight into a forest of evergreens. Brandon slowed to a crawl and drove past. He muttered the number on the roadside mailbox to Troy. "Should I follow?" he asked.

"I'll be there in about ten minutes, I think," Troy said. "Why don't you wait?"

"What if they're bringing her here to—do something to her?" Brandon demanded.

"OK, but don't drive up. They'd spot your headlights."

Brandon pulled onto the narrow shoulder, getting the big truck as far as he could off the road. He turned off the headlights and engine and took the keys with him. After momentary indecision, he took the firearm with him, though he wasn't sure he could use it. Holding it gingerly in both hands, he hurried down the gravel road, which twisted between towering pine trees and led into what looked like pure darkness.

He stumbled along, afraid to use the light on his phone. In a few minutes, lights appeared through the trees. Walking toward them, he saw a sleek modern home at the top of a short rise. In the lights along the overhanging roof of the front porch, the SUV was the only vehicle Brandon saw parked outside.

He crept up the slight incline toward the home. Not seeing anyone guarding it, he climbed the steps to the porch quietly and went toward one of the windows.

"Drop the gun or I'll blow your fucking guts out," a voice said behind him.

# CHAPTER TWENTY-NINE

Brandon froze, his bowels loosening with panic.

"I said drop it, motherfucker," the voice said again. Brandon looked at the gun clutched uselessly in his hands. He crouched down and slowly, cautiously laid it on the porch, then stood up.

"Hands where I can see them," the man behind him said, and Brandon held his hands out from his body, feeling sick.

"Now, open the door," the man said. Brandon obeyed, moving toward the front door. It was unlocked. A hand shoved him between the shoulder blades and he walked unwillingly inside. The man clicked a switch and the room flooded with light from recessed fixtures in the smooth white ceiling. The spacious living area was empty and impeccably clean.

The hand pushed him again. "That way," the man's voice said. It sounded like Yevhen, though Brandon was afraid to look back. He stumbled forward down a short hallway as the man prodded and ordered him forward until he got to a door. Brandon opened it at the man's direction and found himself going down stairs into the basement. The small area at the foot of the stairs was bland and plain except for a heavy-looking door.

"Turn around," the man said tersely, and Brandon did as he was told. He got a look at his captor for the first time. Yevhen broke into a grin when he saw Brandon's face.

"Ah, it *is* you!" he crowed. "The boss's pretty boy. When they called and told me someone had stolen a truck, I hoped it was you from their description, but the whole time I let you follow me I couldn't believe I would get this lucky."

"What—what do you mean?" Brandon asked.

"Oh, there's a big prize on your head," Yevhen said with a nasty smile. "Now turn around, get down on your knees and put your hands behind your head." Brandon's insides turned to ice. He was sure he was about to die, and found himself unable to move.

Yevhen apparently guessed what he was thinking. "Don't worry, pretty boy—boss doesn't want you dead. I would've killed you already if I didn't want the prize. Now turn around and get on the floor like I told you."

Brandon did so weakly, clasping his hands behind his head.

"Now," Yevhen said with satisfaction, "I will show you what I have won. I think you'll like it. I *know* I will."

He moved toward the heavy door. He turned back and pointed his handgun at Brandon. "Remember not to move. I don't want to kill you." Then he tapped a code on a keypad, pulled the door handle down and swung it open.

Brandon had a sinking feeling even before he saw inside the dimly lit room. Nasreen, still hooded and bound, lay on her side on the floor. Another armed man stood guard. Yevhen pushed Brandon into the room and made him resume the same pose as before, then stepped past him to stand over Nasreen's body.

"Go on up and wait for the boss," he told the other man, who nodded and holstered his gun, barely glancing at Brandon as he left.

Yevhen looked down at Nasreen, then back at Brandon. "Yeah, I know, she's not much to look at right now. But once she gets cleaned up, she'll do. And since I caught *you*, I get *her* whenever I want her, for as long as I like." He bent over and pulled the hood roughly off Nasreen's head. She sucked in fresh air with big, gasping breaths. Then she caught sight of who else was there. "Brandon?" she said disbelievingly in a hoarse voice.

He met her eyes. He couldn't believe he had found her, and that it had turned out this way. "I'm sorry," he said. She stared at him, seemingly too stunned for words. "I love you," he added helplessly.

"You love her?" Yevhen said incredulously. "Don't tell me you two were fucking?" Nasreen looked at him with uncomprehending eyes, and Brandon realized she must be heavily sedated, as Troy had guessed. Yevhen shook his head, laughing derisively. "Here I thought she was just your … what's it called? Fag hag. Damn. She needs me more than I thought." He looked down at Nasreen again. "You want to know how your boyfriend was entertaining himself while you were gone?" he said.

Brandon looked at the floor, filled with humiliation. Before Yevhen could say anything more, his phone rang. "Hello?" he said. "Yes boss, everything's under control. Come on in."

Yevhen put his phone back in his pocket, sneering at Nasreen. "Great timing. Now you can meet your old boyfriend's *new* boyfriend."

He held them both at gunpoint where they were. Nasreen lay quietly, and Brandon still knelt with his hands behind his head, too ashamed to meet Nasreen's heavy-lidded eyes, much as he wanted to drink her in. He stared down, his gut clenching with dread at the prospect of seeing Dovzhenko again.

Then they heard feet coming down the stairs. Yevhen opened the door.

"Hi boss," he said cheerily. "Look who I found for you." Brandon heard them approach.

"Excellent work, Yevhen," came the familiar voice. "Well, my dear boy, I didn't expect to see you again today." Brandon felt a hand touching his head; he twisted away from its touch and the same hand dealt him a rough blow. "Hmm, not so agreeable as you were this morning, but you'll come around again soon." Dovzhenko's voice was practically unrecognizable without the ingratiating tone he'd always used with Brandon. "Yevhen, show him his new home. Make him comfortable."

Yevhen gestured with his gun at Brandon. "Get up," he said. For the first time, Brandon focused on the interior of the large room. Chains fastened to the walls and ceiling. A couple of small hard cots against one side of the room. A pile of thin-looking pillows and blankets. Brandon turned to look at Dovzhenko, who stood holding a small pistol. "What are you doing?" he asked, horrified. "What is this place?"

Dovzhenko smirked. "I liked you better when you kept your mouth shut and just did whatever I told you to," he said. "This is my special room. A little while in here and you will be my good boy again." He looked at Yevhen. "I think yours will be more challenging than mine."

Yevhen laughed. "I think I can handle her," he said. He holstered his firearm. "But right now, can you put your gun to her head so her ex-boyfriend doesn't get any ideas?"

Dovzhenko stepped closer to Nasreen's prone body, his gun aimed toward her face. Yevhen saw Brandon's expression and smiled.

"Good, you understand you are not to struggle." He grabbed one of Brandon's unresisting arms at a time, securing them to two manacles connected to chains hanging from the ceiling. Brandon's heart sank even further. He wanted to talk to Nasreen but didn't want to turn the men's attention back to her.

Yevhen finished locking the manacles and spun the key ring around on his finger, then brought it over and dropped it into Dovzhenko's free hand. "Here you go, your pet is safe and sound," he said teasingly. Dovzhenko smiled.

"Excellent work," he said again. "Come, we must call and check that everything has gone well with the other transfers. And then you can claim your prize, and we'll get mine to tell me where we can find his friend."

"I think mine needs to be stripped down and hosed off before I do anything else with her," Yevhen said. Dovzhenko's laughter faded as the heavy door was shut and locked and the two men climbed the stairs.

* * *

The headlights of Brandon's car lit up the back of the box truck, ghostly white in the darkness. Troy sighed with relief.

He pulled up behind it on the shoulder. He regretted not insisting that Brandon wait; he wanted to call or text but was afraid the noise could get him in trouble. Instead, Troy crept through the woods alongside the gravel path until he saw the lights of the house.

He got closer and saw two black SUVs parked in front of it, and two men standing on the porch holding semiautomatic rifles. He circled the building carefully, staying in the shadows, seeing no sign of Brandon. He heard no commotion or activity in the house, nothing but the chirping of crickets and frogs in the woods behind him. Uneasy, he returned to the front of the house where the armed guards stood, found a hiding spot behind a rock among the trees, and waited.

* * *

Left alone with Nasreen, Brandon finally forced himself to look at her again.

"I'm so sorry," he told her, choking up immediately as she looked up at him with eyes that looked huge in her face. "We've been trying so hard to find you. I screwed up and I should have just waited for Troy—he said he'd be here soon, but I didn't want anything to happen to you. I love you so much. I'm sorry I fucked everything up." His voice cracked in a half-sob. "I know you probably can't even understand me right now."

Then she licked her lips and he heard her voice, hoarse and quiet but unmistakable. "Brandon. I do hear you."

# CHAPTER THIRTY

Brandon was stunned. "Nasreen? I—I thought they'd drugged you."

"Not for a while," she said. "I've just been letting them think that." He was amazed at how coherent and composed she sounded, compared with how much worse for the wear she'd seemed when the hood came off. "Do you have a knife or anything sharp on you?"

"No. I had a gun but he made me drop it on the porch." He thought about the contents of his pockets. Wallet, phone, keys … "I do have a lighter," he remembered. He'd hastened to take off the leather jacket when he'd gotten home from his shopping trip with Dovzhenko, but he hadn't thought to get rid of the lighter.

She was silent for a moment. "Can you get to it?"

He tugged at his chains, looked down at his jeans pockets, which seemed a mile away. "No."

"You said Troy would be here soon?"

"I think so," Brandon said hesitantly. "Last time I talked to him, he said he'd get here ten minutes after I did. So as long as he didn't get lost—"

"Which pocket is the lighter in?" she asked.

"Uh, right front," Brandon said, puzzled. "Why?"

Instead of responding, Nasreen stretched her bound hands as far down her back as she could, then wiggled and strained. Brandon watched in amazement as she pulled her hips through the circle of her arms, then tucked her legs to her chest and got her feet through as well. Her hands were still tied but no longer behind her back.

She sat up and fiddled with her ankle bindings, but soon gave up and instead inched over to him and struggled into a kneeling position.

She brought her tied hands up and dug in his right pants pocket, and her slender fingers hooked the gold lighter.

Then she scooted back the way she'd come, toward the pile of bedding in the corner. She flicked the lighter and held it to one of the blankets.

"Try to breathe shallow when the smoke reaches you," she said over her shoulder as she got a corner of a blanket smoldering and moved to another one.

She lit the blankets and pillows in several places, then made her way back to roughly the same spot she'd been lying. Her bound hands were now in front of her, but other than that, she replicated the position she'd been in when Dovzhenko and Yevhen had left.

"Now what?" Brandon asked her, marveling at her composure.

"Now we wait," she said. "Try not to get knocked out by the smoke, but *act* knocked out. If one of them gets close enough to you, kick as hard as you can." She smiled, a ghost of her normal smile, but he still melted. "That's all I could come up with. Let's hope it's enough."

* * *

From his concealed location, Troy heard sudden shouting inside the house. The two guards on the porch conferred briefly and one of them bolted into the house. The other stayed at his post, but for the moment was busy peering in through a window to the right of the door, trying to see what was going on in the house.

Troy took his chance. He streaked up the lawn, pulling his handgun from its holster. His dash up the porch stairs made a sudden clatter and the remaining guard spun around, trying to aim his rifle, but Troy was too close. He knocked the rifle aside and brought the butt of his own gun down on the man's head. The man shuddered but still tried to move his rifle into position, so Troy hit him again, and his eyes rolled back in his head as he crumpled to the porch floor.

Troy holstered his handgun, pried the rifle out of the unconscious man's hands, and tried the front door. Unlocked. He went in and saw no one, but smelled smoke and heard a commotion. He headed toward the short hallway it was coming from.

Just then Dovzhenko burst through a partly opened door, holding his left arm to his nose and coughing violently into his sleeve. He looked up with watery eyes and froze as he saw Troy, standing at the other end of the hallway with a rifle aimed at him.

"Drop it," Troy said evenly. Dovzhenko's gun, which was dangling from his right hand, fell to the floor with a clatter.

* * *

The smoke had started irritating Brandon's lungs almost immediately. He pressed his face into his shirt sleeve, the only thing he could do with his arms chained above his head, and tried to breathe shallowly as Nasreen had instructed. Clad only in the low-cut sleeveless minidress, she had nothing to breathe through, but she tucked her chin down to her chest, lay calmly, and breathed as little as necessary. The smoldering blankets billowed smoke throughout the room.

After what seemed like an interminable length of time, long enough for Brandon to start to think they'd simply suffocate together, they heard the heavy door swing open, and three men came in. Brandon stopped breathing against his sleeve and slumped, hanging limply from his chains with his head bowed, trying to look unconscious. He peered up at the men as best he could. He couldn't see well in the haze with his burning eyes, but he thought he recognized Yevhen, one of the henchmen from the club, and Dovzhenko.

Yevhen rushed over to him, the second man to Nasreen, and Dovzhenko milled about the burning pile of bedding, trying futilely to smother it. He quickly became overwhelmed by the smoke and gave up. "I'll get more help," he choked out between coughs as he left.

Yevhen got closer to Brandon, starting to lift his chin to check on his condition. Without warning, Brandon kicked his knee up as hard as he could into the man's crotch, causing him to double over with a guttural moan of pain. As the other man crouched over Nasreen, she swung her bound hands up and made contact with his chin, then sat up and brought her fists down on top of his head.

Yevhen, who had been holding his handgun, had dropped it with a clatter at his feet while he struggled to get control of his body, and Nasreen flung herself forward onto her belly. Grabbing the gun, she twisted around and shot Yevhen in the head and then turned and fired a bullet through the chest of the other man, who'd already had blood pouring from his mouth, his teeth having clipped his tongue as a result of her first blow. Both men fell to the concrete floor, their dying breaths full of acrid smoke.

The exertion had caused Nasreen to inadvertently breathe deeper and inhale more smoke. Now racked with a hacking cough, she clumsily wriggled toward the door, which Dovzhenko had left ajar in his hurry to get out.

As she faltered, trying to catch her breath, the door flew fully open. Troy stood there brandishing the rifle. After a hasty assessment of the situation, he set the gun down and hugged Nasreen tightly, then half helped, half dragged her partway up the stairs to where the smoke was less severe. He ran back in to where Brandon was, testing the manacles futilely and swearing.

Brandon was coughing too, but he managed to say, "Dovzhenko's got keys."

Troy raced back out the door and up the stairs. He grabbed Nasreen, who seemed to be about to pass out, under the arms and pulled her up into the hallway. Dovzhenko lay a short distance away, a laceration on his forehead, blinking and regaining consciousness.

"Nasreen!" Troy shouted, slapping her cheeks. "Can you watch him while I get

Brandon?" Her eyes cleared somewhat and she nodded yes, raising Yevhen's gun—which she'd kept hold of even as she started to faint—with her still-bound hands. She pointed it at Dovzhenko while Troy rifled through his pockets.

Brandon's eyes and lungs were burning and he was struggling to take breaths. He wasn't sure how long it had been since everyone had left. The fire in the pile of bedding wasn't spreading, but it was still producing clouds of smoke, and Brandon couldn't even see the men on the floor anymore. Despite his panic, he felt his eyelids start to grow heavy as blackness descended around him. Just then, he felt a hand grab one of his wrists and work frantically at something, he couldn't focus on what. That arm dropped limply and Brandon would have collapsed toward the floor, but he fell against someone instead.

Troy supported his weight while he hurriedly unclasped the other manacle. Then he heaved Brandon entirely onto his shoulder, straining with the effort, starting to cough and wheeze himself, and carried him out of the room and up the basement stairs.

# CHAPTER THIRTY-ONE

Nasreen studied Brandon fondly as they lay side by side on stretchers. The ambulance—which had been idling for what felt like hours since they'd been carried in, checked over, and hooked up to oxygen—finally started forward, and the motion woke Brandon from his light slumber.

She could see now why he ordinarily kept his hair cropped so short. He looked like a teenager with the tousled blond curls that had grown in during the past few weeks.

Which made it even harder to think of how he must feel about learning she was involved with another man. And yet, she thought, he'd risked his life to find her.

There was so much to catch up on and deal with, but she felt like she had to get that out of the way first. She breathed deeply of the oxygen, then spoke, her voice hoarse from smoke and muffled by the mask. It took effort, so she got straight to the point.

"Are you mad? About me and Troy?"

Brandon glanced over at the EMT, but he was busy looking through a drawer of plastic-wrapped medical supplies. Brandon's voice too was raspy and faint. "I wish you'd told me."

"I know." Nasreen sighed. "I was going to. But it should've been sooner."

Brandon nodded but seemed preoccupied by some other thought. His gaze skittered away from hers and his voice got even quieter.

"Something ... happened." She waited. He kept his eyes averted. "One night, me and Troy, we ... got together." She saw a flush spread over the half of his face that was visible. "I don't know how ..."

Nasreen's eyes widened. As she struggled to comprehend, her pulse sped up. She'd never seen Troy with a man but she'd thought about it plenty, so it wasn't hard to picture him with Brandon.

"Everything was so crazy," Brandon said tiredly. "I'm sorry."

"No, cutie," she said firmly, despite her surprise.

"I love you," he said, still not looking at her. "I know that's—"

"I love you too." Her words seemed to shock him into silence. "And him." The words hung between them in air that felt thick and heavy with significance.

"Do you ... like him?" she finally asked.

As he hesitated, she tried to read his face, feeling handicapped by the mask obscuring half of it.

Just then the ambulance took a hard right and they both bounced against the straps holding them to their gurneys as it started down what felt like a steep rocky road.

"What's happening?" Nasreen said, as loudly as she could. The effort triggered a coughing fit. The EMT turned toward her and her stomach dropped. She'd seen that face several times before, looming over her in the warehouse.

* * *

The property swarmed with agents, cops, firefighters, and EMTs as Troy gave Agent Koski his statement. The man was detailed and methodical in his questioning even though Troy knew they'd probably repeat everything in an official interview back at headquarters. He employed every ounce of willpower to maintain a calm and reasonable facade, but inside he was straining with impatience and worry. Shortly after Jeff Hanson had left in his car with Dovzhenko and his associate cuffed in the back seat, the ambulance carrying Nasreen and Brandon had pulled away. Their pale faces and labored breathing haunted him; all he wanted was to get to the hospital to be near them.

At last he was allowed to go, with strict instructions to come into headquarters when contacted, and practically bolted through the woods to Brandon's car. He pulled up the hospital address on GPS and let the robotic voice guide him as he processed everything that had happened.

The first responders had arrived quickly from the nearby hospital; the FBI had taken longer, coming from farther away. Firefighters and EMTs had already entered Dovzhenko's home to snuff out the flames, tend to the injured, and confirm the dead when Hanson pulled up.

Troy hadn't been surprised when Hanson seemed to bristle at his attempt to fill him in. Midlevel authorities in any government entity, from the DMV to the Marines, always got defensive when someone stepped into their lane. Troy tried his best to smooth ruffled feathers by staying calm and cooperative. He surrendered his weapon without complaint and refrained from any criticism of the Bureau's slow mobilization. But the scene quickly became an almost comical push and pull of differing opinions over the FBI's power in light of Dovzhenko's diplomatic status.

Dovzhenko was untied, then cuffed, then uncuffed, as Hanson and Koski fought over whether he could be shackled. On the one hand, he wasn't carrying his State Department ID or driving a vehicle with diplomatic plates, so his identity couldn't be officially verified. On the other hand, the FBI had done their research after Troy and Brandon's visit, so they knew very well who Dovzhenko was and his rank.

However, Koski argued, these were extenuating circumstances where not detaining him could enable more crimes to be committed, with the lives of his captives in at least one warehouse in the city hanging in the balance. Then again, Hanson countered, they were taking the word of a man who had broken into an ambassador's home and assaulted him. An ambassador who'd had one of the FBI's own handcuffed and clearly abused in the basement, Koski reminded him.

Troy had watched this jockeying with incredulous anger, glad that Nasreen couldn't see it. After everything she'd gone through—and everything he and Brandon had done to find her—to see the situation deteriorate into a mind-numbing morass of red tape and bureaucratic technicalities was the ultimate outrage.

Koski was trying his best, but as a subordinate there was only so much pushing he could do. Troy had encountered so many useless specimens like Hanson during his military service, who did more harm with their unimaginative fixation on rules than if they'd actually consider pushing boundaries once in a while.

Still, with state troopers also watching the farce, Hanson finally relented and cuffed Dovzhenko's hands before putting him in the back of his car. Troy had felt a growing loathing of Hanson, and he sensed the feeling was mutual.

By contrast, Koski had been refreshingly unhostile during his interview and even expressed some admiration at Troy and Brandon's rogue mission. But by then Troy was beyond impatient.

He tore himself away from this fruitless rehashing of his frustration and checked the time. Nasreen and Brandon should be at the hospital by now. He instructed his phone to call and waded through a menu of options to get to the front desk of the emergency room.

Finding his outer calm just in time, he easily talked the receptionist into looking up their records to see if he could find out anything about their status. "There's no record of them here," she finally said after a minute that seemed like an hour.

"How long should it take for them to get into the system?" he asked.

"Well, the EMTs usually start the process on the way over," she said cautiously, "but sometimes they don't get a chance until they get here. When they do, it's five minutes at most; they can't hand them over until they're in the computer."

Troy hung up abruptly. He stared ahead at the dark road, drumming his fingers on the wheel, occasionally swearing to himself.

His phone buzzed and he glanced at it, nearly swerving off the road when he saw the text that had popped up. He pulled over and looked up where Brandon's phone was located.

Dread paralyzed him for a second or two, no longer. Then he threw the car into drive and made a screeching U-turn.

# CHAPTER THIRTY-TWO

Nasreen tore at her oxygen mask and her restraints, moving quickly despite her coughing, but as she staggered to her feet, bumping her head on the ceiling of the ambulance, Dovzhenko's man stabbed a needle deep into her arm, and she cried hoarsely at the sharp pain.

Undeterred at first, she slammed her knee into his crotch, then gripped his head when he bent in agony, bashing it against the edge of a metal stand.

He fell to the vehicle floor, half-conscious, and a gun clattered out of his stolen uniform.

She grabbed it and fired point blank into his head.

Brandon saw red and mottled gray splattered on the floor. He hadn't been able to see clearly when Nasreen had shot the men in the basement. He froze, unprepared for the sight.

But then she stumbled and fell to her knees, her eyes glassy, as whatever the syringe had contained began to take effect, and Brandon found himself able to move again, freeing himself from the gurney with clumsy movements. He found his phone and shot off a quick text to Troy: 911. It was a long shot whether Troy would even see it, let alone get to them anytime soon, but he had to try.

Next he pulled the half-empty hypodermic from Nasreen's arm, shuddering, and laid it on the metal stand, the corner bloody from the man's scalp. The gun had fallen from Nasreen's limp fingers and Brandon picked it up, the second time that night he'd held a firearm that he had no idea how to use.

And no time to figure it out. The latch on the rear door of the ambulance rattled, and he looked up, his heart in his mouth. He pressed himself against the side, but the space was too small to find a place of concealment.

As the door was flung open, he shouted, hoping the shakiness of his voice wasn't obvious through the hoarseness of smoke damage. "Stay back or I'll shoot!" He suppressed a coughing fit and held the gun in what he prayed was a convincingly threatening way.

He couldn't see who had opened the door. All was dark outside. Then the unseen man spoke.

"Don't do this. You don't want to shoot anyone."

He pressed his lips together, trying to gain control of his voice. "Why are *you* doing this? Dovzhenko's going down. It's over."

"I wouldn't be so sure of that," the voice said, sounding amused. "Let's make a deal. Come out now and I won't kill you. Maybe boss will still want you alive. At least you will have a chance."

Brandon's gut lurched. He didn't know how he would shoot the man anyway; he couldn't see him and had no idea how to fire the gun. He lowered it reluctantly to the floor, blood pounding in his ears, expecting the unseen figure to shoot him at any moment.

"That's good. Now come on out of there." No, he wasn't planning to kill him, at least not right away. Brandon moved toward the opening, stooped over in the low-ceilinged vehicle. He swayed unsteadily, the burning in his lungs demanding his attention, and reached out for balance. As his hand fell on the metal tray, he felt the syringe, and his fingers closed around it of their own accord.

"Hurry up," the voice ordered, sounding less amused. "Get out here now."

Brandon took one hesitant step after another until he'd reached the edge, then stepped onto the grass, struggling to adjust his eyes to the darkness as he strained to see his adversary.

An arm locked around his neck from behind, and his burning throat felt a wave of fresh pain as the vicelike grip blocked his air passage. Spots appeared before his eyes. He stumbled back against the man, found the end of the syringe with his thumb, and thrust backward as hard as he could manage. He connected; the needle pierced cloth and sank deep into the man's thigh, and Brandon squeezed the remaining contents into his flesh.

Surprised, the man lost his balance and fell back, taking Brandon with him. Brandon heard a grunt as he landed hard on the man's chest and stomach, knocking the air out of him.

The arm around his neck was gone and he rolled off, scrabbling away on his hands and knees. He hit a baseball-sized rock with the heel of his right hand and grabbed it, ignoring the pain.

Turning back, he saw the man struggling to his feet. He didn't see a gun but expected one to go off at any moment. Desperately he raised his right fist and brought the rock down on the man's head. He fell back and Brandon hit him again, and again. He heard a crunching sound and the man went completely still.

He felt wetness on his hand and brought it up, seeing dark patches against his pale skin in the faint light from the ambulance. He stared at it with horror. "I'm sorry," he whispered faintly, but there was no one to hear.

In the distance, a car approached, engine gunning.

# CHAPTER THIRTY-THREE

Brandon staggered weakly to his feet and climbed into the back of the ambulance. He reached Nasreen and patted her cheeks. "Come on, come on," he muttered.

When she didn't respond, he gripped her under the arms and dragged her painstakingly through the litter of medical supplies scattered on the floor. He pulled her clumsily out of the ambulance, then, inch by inch, under the vehicle.

He heard a car door slam and the rustle of approaching feet through the undergrowth. He focused on getting Nasreen as far under the ambulance as he could, as quietly as he could, hoping they would be out of sight when more of Dovzhenko's men arrived.

He heard steps around him, sounds of movement as the vehicle and the dead men were inspected. Then a man said, as if to himself, "Fuck. Where are they?"

It took Brandon a second to find his own voice, he was so overcome with relief. "We're here." He scrambled on his belly out from under the ambulance and looked up into Troy's face.

* * *

Together, the two men carried Nasreen up to the road and laid her across the back seat of Brandon's car. She was unconscious, but her breathing was steady and her eyelids fluttered occasionally.

Troy once again directed his GPS to lead them to the hospital. They'd thought about using the ambulance but weren't sure it would make it back up the steep incline—and they didn't relish the idea of putting Nasreen near the dead body there, or moving the body, or any of the scenarios that surfaced.

Brandon sat in the front passenger seat, turned halfway so he could keep an eye on Nasreen, his arm stretched to hold her limp hand gently in his. He could hardly believe he was touching her again. Troy fixed his eyes on the road, lost in thought.

"How are they always one step ahead of us?" he said finally. Brandon tore his eyes away from Nasreen. Troy shook his head as he sifted through ideas.

"What do you mean?" Brandon finally asked.

"We were doing fine at first," Troy mused. "Dovzhenko had no idea you were after him—if so, he'd never have let you out of his apartment last night. When he saw you this morning, he let you go again. Went to the warehouse, planned the shipment—business as usual for him. Then all of a sudden, he starts moving his prisoners out. He takes Nasreen to his place. What changed?"

"Yevhen wasn't surprised when he found me on the porch," Brandon said with sudden wonder. "Why not? Why'd he think I'd be there?"

"And how did Dovzhenko's men take over the ambulance?" Troy added. "Were they coming up to the house anyway—or did someone tell them to come?"

"The guy I—killed," Brandon said, forcing the last word out painfully. "He said he didn't think Dovzhenko was finished. He sounded really confident. What happened to him after I went in the ambulance?"

"Hanson took him to headquarters," Troy said. He was silent for a few beats. "There was this fucked-up, ridiculous thing between him and Koski. He kept arguing that no one should be in the house because it belonged to a diplomat. And that Dovzhenko shouldn't be in handcuffs. But eventually Koski won him over."

"Did anyone go with Hanson?" Brandon asked.

"No," Troy said, almost absently. "Just the other guy I'd tied up."

Going back over everything in his mind, Brandon gasped. "He knew I knew Nasreen," he blurted. "Dovzhenko. And Yevhen knew I'd recognize her when he pulled the hood off. How did they—"

"Hanson." Troy's voice had a snarl to it that Brandon had never heard before. "Has to be. It's either him or someone else in the Bureau, but the way he was interfering with everything … It's Hanson." He swore again and pounded the steering wheel. "Find an airport," he told Brandon.

Brandon took his phone out hesitantly. "What am I—"

"An airport!" Troy repeated. "Where else would Dovzhenko want Hanson to take him? He's gotta get out of the country before Ukraine yanks his immunity. Look for small private ones close by."

"Leary." Nasreen's voice, hoarse and tired, from the back seat. Brandon turned to see her struggling to sit up. Relief mingled with confusion.

"What?"

"The airport he uses for charter flights," she said. "Look it up. Gotta be close."

# CHAPTER THIRTY-FOUR

Dovzhenko looked at his faint reflection in the car window and dabbed at the blood on his face, scraping dried bits with his fingernail. Not that any pilot at Leary would ask questions, but he wanted to sound as few alarm bells as possible. "Take the next right," he instructed.

Hanson's eyes met his in the rearview mirror. The agent's face looked sweaty and pale even in the dark. "You're sure they'll be ready to take off when we get there." The coward never expected his life to go in this direction. *Well, neither did I,* Dovzhenko thought grimly. As usual, he'd have to clean up after incompetent subordinates.

"Always," Dovzhenko answered curtly, suppressing a sneer at the wild-eyed terror on the man's face. He knew he had to play nice a while longer. He'd promised to take Hanson with him. How long they traveled together would depend on how long he'd remain useful. Dovzhenko imagined that usefulness would hit its limit fairly soon, but right now, Hanson was absolutely vital to his escape. He refolded his handkerchief and went back to wiping rather fruitlessly at the smears of blood.

* * *

The lights of the short airstrip and the building next to it appeared out of the darkness. The area was otherwise deserted and the road sporadically lit, so their destination was easy to spot.

A small plane idled on the runway, and Brandon saw three figures walking up the stairs into the open door. "There they are!"

Troy sped toward the airport and reached the parking lot just as the plane began taxiing away from them. A chain-link fence separated the parking area from the tarmac, and Troy gunned the engine, heading straight for it. "Get your head down," he told Brandon. He ducked, covering his head with both arms as his little car smashed into the fence at full speed.

Brandon looked up when the car bumped over the downed chain-link and began to pick up speed again. They were gaining quickly on the plane, which was moving into position at one end of the runway.

"Go past it," Nasreen said. She'd spoken very little, saving her strength, but when Brandon looked back at her this time, she was leaning forward, her eyes fixed on the plane and her mouth set tensely. "Do you have a gun?" she asked.

Troy pulled one out of the drink holder on the driver side door and held it over his shoulder, never taking his eyes off the plane.

"Picked this up in the ambulance—don't know if it's loaded."

Nasreen actually smiled as she took it. "Should be—I only fired it once." Brandon couldn't believe her composure. They passed the plane; the roar of the propellers was disconcertingly loud and close to Brandon's window. "Get ready," she instructed Troy. "OK—now!"

He screeched to a stop, the car swerving into the path of the plane. Nasreen threw open the back door of the car and leapt out before Brandon knew what was happening. She planted her feet and squared her shoulders as the plane bore down on them. The two men were frozen in the front seat.

She aimed and fired, squeezing off one shot after another. Bullets hit the windshield, glancing off it but leaving frosty circles of damaged glass. With awful clarity, Brandon saw Dovzhenko behind the pilot, pounding his shoulder as if urging him on. But the aircraft mercifully veered to the right, barely missing the car, and slowed to a halt.

* * *

It was a reunion of sorts as police, ambulances, and FBI descended on the tiny airport. Hanson, Dovzhenko, and his henchman had failed to threaten the pilot into restarting takeoff.

They stayed in the plane until ordered out by the first authorities to arrive—Koski and a team of agents. When Troy had called him, he wasted no time coming—the real EMTs' bodies had been discovered and he'd had agents combing the area already for the stolen vehicle.

Brandon watched Dovzhenko carefully as he was cuffed and placed into the back of a car. His body seemed smaller, deflated. Hanson and the other prisoner were taken in a separate vehicle. As the cars pulled away, Brandon felt a slight sense of relief, but it was hard to trust it.

This time, with Koski in charge, the scene was orderly and things moved quickly. Nasreen refused to get in the new ambulance that had come. "We'll get ourselves to the hospital," she said firmly, and Koski didn't argue. He had more than enough to worry about with a crooked superior, a diplomat in custody, and warehouses full of captives to rescue.

Troy got back in the driver's seat out of habit. Brandon opened the front passenger door and helped Nasreen in, and he climbed in back. The car pulled away, leaving the flashing lights behind and heading out onto the darkened road.

Only one headlight was working after their collision with the chain-link fence, and the windshield was spiderwebbed with cracks. Nasreen and Troy were murmuring softly to one another, and some part of the vehicle was making a worrisome squeaking noise, but other than that it was quiet in the car.

Brandon wondered what they were talking about, but his mind was crowded with other thoughts, reeling with disbelief as he relived the day's events, and his body was tensed as if it expected something else to take them by surprise.

"Is it over?" Brandon asked, half to himself. They passed a streetlight and its illumination slid through the car. He saw Troy's and

Nasreen's hands clasped between the seats, and his own question took on a different meaning in his mind. He closed his eyes, feeling a mixture of pain and acceptance wash over him.

Then he felt something else—a light touch on the back of his hand. He opened his eyes. Nasreen was smiling at him. She was here, she was safe—the miracle of it hit him all over again.

He was even more incredulous when she took his hand and drew it toward her. He leaned forward and she placed his hand on Troy's. The man's strong fingers interlaced with Brandon's, and Nasreen cupped her hand over theirs. Brandon's heart skipped a beat.

"I don't know, cutie," she said. "I think that's up to you."

# AFTERWORD

A few notes about the geography of *Devil's Sanctum*:

I knew the settings and actions I wanted for my novel, and I went in search of real-life equivalents. If I didn't find one, I took generous liberties. For example, I wanted my characters to encounter a Ukrainian neighborhood in D.C. In my research I found Ukrainian culture and heritage sprinkled here and there in D.C. and Maryland, but not a concentrated neighborhood, so I created Little Odessa.

As for Seattle, I did some internet tourism and incorporated real landmarks into the scenes there, but the vast majority of places are made up. (I did have several readers familiar with Seattle confirm my fictional settings didn't seem out of line with the city.)

Speaking of Ukraine: I knew I wanted a diplomat from another country to figure largely in my book, and I thought I'd chosen one with a relatively low news profile. Then,

during editing, impeachment happened, and
Ukraine dominated headlines. But I decided to
keep it because if I'd switched countries, the
same thing could easily happen at some point,
and creating a fictional country would take
readers too far out of the real world.

# ACKNOWLEDGMENTS

The current form of this novel wouldn't have been possible without the attentive review and excellent insights of my beta readers. They helped me bring out aspects of my characters that were in my head but hadn't made it onto the page, and I'm grateful to them for helping me infuse more life into *Devil's Sanctum*. Emily, Stevie, and Jaclyn: Thank you from the bottom of my heart!

COMING SOON FROM T.A. BERKELEY

*Eternal Order*

Fresh out of the academy, police detective Lyndon Bates is eager for his first big assignment. But he couldn't imagine how big it was going to be: Investigating the murder of Crenshaw Connelly, the galaxy's biggest reality star, on the grounds of a secretive religious order on another planet. And there's a catch: Only women are allowed inside.

Lyndon leaves his body behind and ventures onto planet Halcyon as a woman. She soon realizes the question of who killed Crenshaw is only one of the mysteries lurking within the walls of this heavenly convent, where no one seems to age, and Lyndon isn't alone in not being what she seems.

*The Infinity Cure*

It's a gala like no other. A wealthy philanthropist has brought the best scientific minds and deep-pocketed donors together at her underwater estate for a summit to try to solve one of Earth's most pressing crises: A deadly epidemic sweeping through the ancient aquean people, who have called the ocean home for longer than humans have existed. And veteran reporter Hiroe Anno is determined to capture the story for her news service—even if it means overcoming her intense phobia of being in water.

Then, guests start disappearing, and a young aquean poet pulls Hiroe—and her estranged mentor from a rival news service—into an investigation where each disturbing discovery seems to raise a million new questions—about their hostess, the nature of the virus, and the search for the cure.